Sallie Fox

The Story of a Pioneer Girl

By
Dorothy Kupcha Leland

Cover design and illustrations by Diane Wilde

Tomato Enterprises
Davis, California

Sallie Fox: The Story of a Pioneer Girl
By Dorothy Kupcha Leland

Published by:
Tomato Enterprises
P.O. Box 73892
Davis, CA 95616
(916) 750-1832

All rights reserved. No part of this book may be reproduced or transmitted in any form or by any means, electronic or mechanical, including photocopying, recording or by any information storage and retrieval system without written permission from the author, except for the inclusion of brief quotations in a review.

Copyright © 1995 by Dorothy Kupcha Leland

Printed in the United States of America

Library of Congress Catalog Number: 95-061289

Publisher's Cataloging in Publication
(Prepared by Quality Books Inc.)

Leland, Dorothy Kupcha.
    Sallie Fox: the story of a pioneer girl/Dorothy Kupcha Leland. --Davis, CA: Tomato Enterprises, 1995.
    p. cm.
    ISBN 0-9617357-6-7

    1. Fox, Sallie--Juvenile fiction. 2. Frontier and pioneer life--Juvenile fiction.   I. Title
PZ7.L453Sal 1995   813'.54
                                          QBI95-20371

TABLE OF CONTENTS

Sallie's Journey

Dedication:

To Bob, Jeremy, and Rachel

This is a historical novel, based on a true story. Sallie Fox really lived, and the major events of this book really happened. However, minor elements have been fictionalized to provide a smooth story line.

Sallie Fox at age sixteen,
about three years after reaching California.

1. COTTONWOOD CREEK

Sallie plucked a succulent raspberry off the bush and popped it in her mouth. Its tart sweetness tasted so good after weeks of eating mostly salt pork and corn fritters!

"Sallie Fox! You're putting more berries in your mouth than in your bucket," teased her older sister Francie. "What about that cobbler we promised to make for the whole wagon train?"

Ignoring her sister, Sallie ate another berry, and another, and then sighed contentedly. "I haven't eaten anything so tasty since we left Iowa!" she declared. "Won't Father be thrilled when we serve him his favorite dessert?"

Francie looked up and frowned. "Not if we don't make it back to the wagons before dark. We'd better get going before Mama sends the cattle hands out to look for us."

Sallie looked around, startled. She'd been so busy gathering berries, she hadn't noticed how far they'd wandered. Here, the river bank was much steeper and muddier than where they had previously scrambled down to the water's edge.

"This looks hard to climb," Sallie said. "Should we go back the way we came?"

"That will take too long," replied Francie. "I don't want Mama to worry about us."

Just then, Sallie screamed. There, on the ground, not two feet from her, was the largest snake she had ever seen! She leapt backwards, crashing into her sister. Both went sprawling on the muddy ground. They just missed falling into Cottonwood Creek itself.

Frozen with fear, and clinging to her sister, Sallie watched as the snake hissed and flicked its tongue. After what seemed an eternity, it finally uncoiled and slithered into the underbrush.

"It's gone," Francie whispered. "Let's get out of here!"

They tried climbing the steep river bank, but both slid back in the mud. Some of the precious berries spilled out of the buckets, but they saved most of them.

"Don't you think we'd better go back the old way?" asked Sallie.

Francie shook her head. "No. The snake went that way. I'm going this way." She charged back up the muddy slope and somehow made it to the top this time.

But Sallie couldn't get her footing. Plastered with mud, she grew panicky. "Help me, Francie! I just know that snake is coming back to get me, and it's too dark to see anything down here!"

"Hold on, Sallie," Francie called. "I'm looking for a long stick." She rummaged through some nearby bushes, broke off a suitable branch, and handed it down to Sallie. Slowly, she pulled her sister up the muddy bank.

At the top, Sallie paused to catch her breath. Then, with her bucket in one hand and her muddy skirt in the other, she raced after Francie towards the circle of wagons.

When they reached camp, dusk had faded to darkness. In the firelight, Sallie's mother stirred a big pot of stew. The girls put down their buckets and stood quietly in front of her.

Mama glared at them. *"Where have you been?* You know Father's rules. All children inside the circle after dark! And look at you, covered with mud from head to foot!"

Sallie bit her lip and looked down miserably at her muddy dress and boots. Knowing she had let Mama down prompted two tears to roll down her dirty cheeks and fall off the end of her chin. "I'm sorry, Mama," she whispered.

"When I gave you permission to pick berries, you promised to be back before dark," Mama continued sternly. "Fixing dinner for all these hungry men and you five children is burden enough. I can't be worrying that two of my girls have been carried off by Indians!"

Then Mama's voice softened, and she gave them each a small hug, being careful not to get mud on herself. "I'm glad you're safe. Now, let's get you two cleaned up, and find a good pot for that cobbler!"

Before dawn the next morning, Sallie awoke with a start and sat bolt upright in the covered wagon. Her heart pounded, and it took her a moment to get her bearings. Then she realized where she was, and heaved a sigh of relief, whispering, "Oh, it was only a dream about yesterday."

Sniffing the welcome scent of frying bacon, she poked her head out of the wagon. There, she saw what she saw every morning on the trail: Mama, Francie, and Liefy, cooking breakfast in the dark. Taking care not to wake Julia, still slumbering next to her, Sallie threw aside the warmth of her quilt and reached for her clothes. She knew the blue checked gingham dress she'd washed the night before would still be wet, so she brought out her spare, a green calico. Next she pulled on the brown leather boots Mama had made her clean so carefully the night before. Scrambling out of the wagon, she hurried over to Francie, squatting next to the fire deftly flipping corn cakes. Meanwhile, Mama poured steaming coffee into metal mugs.

"I dreamed about the snake!" Sallie cried. "I couldn't get up the cliff, and it kept coming after me! I couldn't get away!"

"Don't bother your head about that old snake, Sallie," her sister answered. "He's far away from us now. Here, eat this."

Taking the plate her sister handed her, Sallie said, "But it seemed so real!"

Her mother placed a firm hand on Sallie's shoulder. "Sarah, the time for talking is when the wagons are moving."

Sallie knew Mama meant business when she called her "Sarah." She ate quickly, and then took down the tent where Mama, Father, and little Orrin slept every night. Francie had already scooped up the still-sleeping two-year-old in his little nest of quilts, and put him next to Julia in the wagon. Sallie placed the family's tent and blankets around the two sleeping children. Francie and Liefy washed and packed away the metal plates and cooking utensils. Mama, like the women in the other wagons, made sure everything was properly stored away. In the meantime, the men returned from tending livestock and hitched up the oxen. After a quick head count of the children, the wagons rolled westward, as the light of dawn crept into the eastern sky behind them.

As they pulled away from Cottonwood Creek, Sallie remembered something she had meant to do the night before. Reaching into a small cloth bag she always kept near her in the wagon, she brought out the slim leather bound notebook Aunt Rachel had given her as a going-away present. She opened it and carefully wrote in pencil, "*May 10, 1858. Cottonwood Creek. Raspberries. Snake.*"

2. PRAIRIE DAYS

Sallie was pleased to have a diary entry for every day since they had left Keosauqua, Iowa, five weeks before. Keeping a diary seemed like a very grown up thing to do, but of course she was already twelve—almost thirteen. Someday, she would tell her own children stories about crossing the plains, just as Father had always told them about the Gold Rush.

She looked up from the book in her lap and stared out the front of the wagon. Mama, Francie, and Liefy were all knitting, but Sallie didn't have patience for such handwork. For a while, she watched the oxen plodding in front of her.

Alongside the wagon walked Will Harper, cracking his rawhide whip over the backs of the animals, shouting commands. The popper at the end of his whip rarely touched the oxen. Its sound alone, like a pistol shot, spurred them on. Will was older—at least twenty—and one of Father's helpers.

Sallie surveyed the surrounding prairie and murmured, "It's different here. Flatter, and the grass is shorter." Perhaps she would write that in her diary, too.

Without looking up from her knitting, Francie replied, "Father says we won't see rolling, long grass prairie again for the rest of our trip. Just flat land like this, and then desert until Santa Fe. Then mountains and more desert 'til California."

Prairie. Desert. Santa Fe. California. The words conjured up such strange images in Sallie's mind. Before this trip, she couldn't remember ever leaving Van Buren County, Iowa. Yet, here she was on the Santa Fe Trail, heading to the magical land Father had talked about since she was four years old! But, while the idea of California was exciting, Sallie found actually getting there long, tedious, and uncomfortable. The past five weeks had already seemed like a lifetime, and their trip had barely begun!

When Sallie closed her eyes, she could easily picture the home she'd left behind: their two-room log cabin, the surrounding farmlands, the big beautiful walnut tree in Uncle Charles' front yard. It was much harder to imagine a new life in California, though Aunt Julia had sent Mama letters filled with vivid descriptions.

To pass the time, Sallie turned back to the beginning of the diary in her lap, and read its very first entry. *"April 3, 1858. Left Keosauqua to go west. With luck, I shall see California before my thirteenth birthday."* Then she read through the rest of the short entries, recalling how their wagons had wound through the small towns and farms of southern Iowa and Missouri, crossed the Missouri River by ferryboat, and rolled across the beautiful untamed prairie of Kansas Territory.

Those first few days in Kansas had seemed like a fantasy! Wildflowers of all colors had blanketed the prairie. *It looks just like the Persian rug in Aunt Rachel's living room back home,* Sallie had written in her diary. She and her sisters had spent hours gathering huge bunches of the colorful flowers, and twisting them into garlands. The girls wore them in their hair and around their waists, and even decorated the wagon with them.

After ten days in Kansas, they had reached Council Grove, a settlement with a few stores and houses. Father had said it was the last chance to buy supplies, and the last place to cut timber hard enough for spare wagon parts. "Take a good look around," he'd told them. "You won't see another town till we reach New Mexico, at least six weeks from now."

As their wagons had lumbered through Council Grove, Sallie had watched wide-eyed as a small cluster of Indians gathered on the outskirts of town. They sat on the grass in a circle, looking solemn. Their dark hair hung down around their shoulders and they wore plain, simple clothing. Finding such ordinary-looking Indians both relieved and disappointed Sallie. They were not at all what she had imagined Indians to be! Where were the feather headdresses and bright war paint? That day, Sallie had written: *"Council Grove. Father says now we're in Indian country. We must constantly be on our guard."*

Interrupting Sallie's reverie, Mama set aside her knitting. "I've had as much bumping around as I can take right now! I'm ready to stretch my legs." Mama then hitched her skirts up around her knees and jumped out of the slow-moving wagon.

"Me, too!" Francie said, and immediately followed her.

Liefy, however, continued to knit. "My leg's rather hurting today, Sallie," she said softly. "You go. I'll stay here with the little ones." Sallie knew this wagon trip was especially hard on her eighteen-year-old stepsister. A childhood disease had left Relief Brown with a limp and fragile health. Yet despite her physical weakness, Liefy possessed a quiet strength Sallie found comforting. The two had developed a special bond in recent years, and Sallie was glad Relief had finally agreed to come west with them.

"Do you want me to rub your leg for you?"

Liefy shook her head and gave Sallie a gentle smile. "No, really, I'm fine. You go on with Mama and Francie."

Sallie put her diary and pencil back in their brown cloth bag, then jumped out of the wagon herself. She fell into an easy stride with Mama and Francie. It felt good to move her legs!

From this vantage point, Sallie could see the whole wagon train stretched out along the prairie. Looking ahead, she saw the Rose family wagon leading the way. Lawrence Rose was principal owner of this wagon train, which earned him the right to ride up front. Sallie learned from experience why first place was such an enviable position. People riding in the lead didn't have to breathe the dust kicked up by a wagon and team in front of them!

The wagon carrying Sallie's family always came next. Alpha Brown, Sallie's stepfather, was Mr. Rose's foreman, in charge of organizing the wagon train and keeping things running smoothly. Father never rode with the family. He always went on horseback, supervising not only the wagons, but also the young men herding their cattle. Next in line came their three prairie schooners loaded with supplies, followed by a variety of wagons carrying families they had met near the Missouri state line.

Looking over her shoulder, Sallie could see that most of the adults and older children from the other wagons were on foot now, too. Sometimes Sallie dropped back to walk and visit with people from the other wagons, but today she stayed with Mama and Francie. "Oh, Mama," she said, "tell us again about our relatives in California!" Sallie loved hearing family stories.

Mama smiled. "Well, there's your Uncle George, my brother. And Aunt Julia, my sister, and her husband and children. And Aunt Livinia—Vini—one of my other sisters. We shouldn't lack for family out there!"

"And do they all live together?" Sallie asked.

"Vini and George do. She keeps house for him in Placer-ville, in the hills up near the gold mines. Unless, of course, she's found herself a husband by now! Julia and her husband, Josiah Allison, have a farm in a place called Vacaville. I'm told that's rather near San Francisco." Mama's other brother, Charles, and her sister, Harriet, still lived in Iowa.

This got Mama talking about her girlhood in Marietta, Ohio, and how, at nineteen, she'd met and married a handsome young farmer named Aaron Moses Fox. Francie was born the year after they'd married, and Sallie three years later. "He was a good man, Sallie," said Mama, with a sudden look of wistfulness, "and he loved you two girls very much."

Aaron Fox was thrown from a horse and died when Sallie was just a few months old. Mama took Francie and Sallie to Iowa, where the rest of her family had recently moved. For two years, they had lived with Aunt Julia and Uncle Si. It was there Mama met and married Alpha Brown.

"We had quite a wedding, Sallie," Mama reminisced. "It was December 1, 1847. You were the same age little Orrin is now. You and Francie and I, along with Julia's family, were already at the farmhouse. Snow was piled so deep, we didn't know if Alpha and the others could even get there! Suddenly, we heard horses, and here came two big sled loads of people from Keosauqua—Alpha, of course, with Mary Ann and Liefy; the minister and his wife; Uncle Charles and Aunt Rachel, Uncle George, Aunt Vini, Aunt Harriet, and some other friends from town. After the wedding supper, it snowed so hard no one could go home. The whole group spent our wedding night in that two-room log cabin!"

Sallie had no memories of that day, but Frances, who had been five, said she remembered the raisin cake Aunt Julia had made. "And I remember the day after the wedding, when we moved into Father's log cabin in Keosauqua." Francie laughed. "I had to sleep in the same bed with Mary Ann and Liefy, and I didn't want to!"

Father's two daughters from his first marriage, Mary Ann and Relief, had been age ten and eight at the time of the wedding. It had taken a while for the four girls to get used to one another—Mary Ann and Liefy still desperately missed their mother, who had died only the year before. And Francie, who had grown quite attached to Aunt Julia's family, found adjusting to their new living situation quite difficult as well. "Luckily, you girls finally figured out how to get along," Mama mused aloud. "Or I don't know how I would have survived that year Father left us to go searching for gold!"

Mama's storytelling ended when the wagons stopped for nooning—the mid-day break—next to a small stream. Sallie and Francie immediately took water buckets down to the water's edge to fill them. Women and children from other wagons did the same. It was essential to collect drinking water before the men unyoked the animals and brought them down to the stream. Sixty thirsty, dusty oxen and mules would befoul the water supply in a very short time.

The cool shade by the water felt so good! Sallie wanted to soak her feet, but knew that must wait. After filling their buckets, she and Francie hurried back to help prepare the day's cold lunch. They never built fires during this mid-day break. Nooning gave both people and livestock a chance to rest and eat at the hottest part of the day. Will Harper and the other men who drove the oxen were especially exhausted, having walked since daybreak without rest. After a hasty meal, these men lay down, covered their eyes with their hats, and fell asleep.

Sallie rested, but rarely slept, during nooning. For one thing, it was a chance to see Father. After checking on the herd, grazing a comfortable distance from the wagons, he rode his horse over to join the family for lunch. Today, he dismounted from his horse and spoke briefly with Mr. Rose. "Two of the horses developed saddle galls, Lawrence, so we switched them with two of the extras," Father reported. "Other than that, everything's going well."

After lunch, Father sat in the shade of the wagon, and brought out his precious copy of *Commerce of the Prairies*, by Josiah Gregg. He held it as reverently as the Holy Bible itself. Written by a man who had crossed the Santa Fe Trail many times by wagon train, the book offered detailed information and advice for travelers. Father studied it religiously everyday. Today, he read part of it aloud and then said, "This man *knows* what he's talking about. He's one reason this trip is going so well."

"But, Father," seven-year-old Julia piped up. "You don't need that old book to tell you what to do. You've been to

California and back, and you know everything there is to know about wagon trains. I heard Mr. Rose say so!"

Father patted Julia on the head. "That's very flattering, my dear," he said. "But the foremost lesson I've learned on the plains is the importance of being well-prepared."

Sallie smiled as she listened. With Father in charge, she felt sure nothing bad could ever happen!

3. PATIENCE AND PERSEVERANCE

Tedious day after tedious day, the wagon train followed its predictable routine: on the road at daybreak, a cold lunch and a rest at noon, back on the trail until evening. On hot days, Sallie's skin, hair, and clothing became caked with dust and perspiration. Mosquitos and gnats buzzed around her ears, and her mouth always felt dry. Orrin whimpered and whined often, and Sallie knew Mama expected her to help keep him quiet. She did what she could, but was too hot and uncomfortable herself to do much to distract the fussy toddler. Cold days were easier. Sallie would snuggle Orrin on her lap, and Liefy would wrap a blanket completely around the two of them.

Sometimes, frightening thunderstorms came up without warning. Suddenly, the sky would darken as great streaks of lightning forked across it. Huge claps of thunder reverberated across the prairie, sounding to Sallie like the voice of Almighty God himself. Drenching rain pelted the wagons with a fierce intensity, and the ground beneath them—now thick mud—became impassable.

PATIENCE AND PERSEVERANCE

Will Harper would turn the wagon so the animals had their backs to the storm. Then he would seek shelter with Sallie's family, and together they would tighten the wagon cover. Even so, a fine white mist would penetrate the canvas, coating everyone's hair with small drops of water. As the elements roared about them, Liefy and Francie would lead the others in song, and through it all, Mama would calmly knit. Then, as quickly as it had appeared, the storm would pass. As the sun came out, the men would turn the wagons westward again, urging the oxen through the mud.

"How will we ever even get to Santa Fe, let alone California, if we keep getting bogged down in the rain?" Sallie complained to Francie after one such storm.

Her sister shrugged. "Father says once we start crossing the desert, we'll *pray* for rain like this."

Sallie did her best to keep a cheerful attitude, but often succumbed to bouts of frustration.

"*When* will we stop for nooning?" she lamented loudly one hot day. "I'm thirsty, and the water flask is empty!"

She leaned out the back of the wagon and looked despairingly at Mama, Francie, and Liefy, who trudged steadily along in silence. Sallie moaned for extra effect, then had to hastily steady herself, as a sudden lurch of the wagon bounced her skyward. "Mama," she wailed. "I am so sore, and so tired, and so bored! I don't think we'll *ever* reach California!"

"Sarah..." Mama sighed wearily, fixing a steady gaze on her daughter. "We've been through this before. I need you to be strong, Sarah, for the little ones. I'm counting on you to help keep their spirits up. Complaining doesn't help us go faster."

Sallie buried her head in her arms, knocking off her sunbonnet. As it fell from the wagon to the ground, Liefy retrieved it. "Come, Sallie, hop down and walk with me awhile," her stepsister said. "Nooning will be here soon enough."

Sallie clambered out the back of the wagon, and dropped to the ground. Liefy retied Sallie's bonnet, and put a loving hand on her shoulder. "Patience and perseverance, Sallie."

"Patience and perseverance" were two very familiar words to Sallie. Father said them whenever he talked about his rugged trip across the plains in 1849. Mother said them when asked how she survived that difficult year alone with the children when her husband had gone searching for gold. And now, Liefy echoed them, too.

Sallie had only dim memories of the year Father had left them all to look for gold in California. But she had grown up hearing stories about "gold fever" and the thousands of "Forty-niners" who had streamed across the continent in search of instant wealth. A fortunate few had struck it rich. But, most, including Father, had not. After no luck finding gold, he had returned to the family, richer only in experience.

But the lure of California continued to tug at him. He told Sallie and her sisters every detail: the arduous journey across the plains, the brawling, rough life in the mining camps, the beautiful countryside and rich farmland. "It's the land of opportunity," Father told the girls often, "and someday we will all go there together!"

Father was not the only person Sallie had heard talking about California. The summer she had turned seven, Aunt Julia and Uncle Si had sold their Keosauqua land and headed west themselves. Once there, they had established a farm in the rich agricultural lands of Solano County, east of San Francisco. Glowing letters about their new life encouraged George and Vini Baldwin, Mama's brother and sister, to follow them.

Every time Mama received another letter from Aunt Julia, Sallie sensed how much her parents wanted to go west themselves. But could they ever afford it? Moving an entire family took money—for a wagon, oxen, food, and equipment. Sallie's family didn't have much money.

Then, right before Christmas, 1856, Sallie accompanied Father to Lawrence Rose's store—a trip that would change their lives. As Sallie eyed some peppermint candy sticks on the store's counter, she heard Mr. Rose ask Father, "Alpha, if you were to go California again, what would you do differently?"

Without hesitation, Father forcefully replied, "I'd bring the gold with me! Good Iowa cattle would command a hefty price out west, giving me capital to establish myself in a business—maybe ranching."

"Ah, yes," Mr. Rose replied. "I myself started in business by trading cattle. It gave me the nest egg to open this store!"

To Sallie's surprise, Mr. Rose said he wanted to sell his store, and open a horse racing ranch in California. She knew he was already a rich man at age thirty, fifteen years younger than Father.

"I have the cash to finance a wagon expedition west, Alpha, but I have no experience with such a thing," Mr. Rose continued. "Can I hire you to lead my wagon train?"

Sallie still remembered the look of fervent determination in Father's eyes all the way home from the store that day. When they returned home, he told Mama and the others about Mr. Rose's proposal. "We'll drive a herd of Red Durham cattle to California, sell it when we get there, and divide the proceeds. The better the shape of the cattle, the better price they will fetch, and the more money I'll be paid!" Sallie and her sisters had danced with joy that night. They were going to California, and a wonderful new life there, just as Father had always promised!

As the time neared for their departure, Sallie's family moved to a farm outside Keosauqua to grow forage for the cattle and prepare for the trip. Using Mr. Rose's money, Father bought and outfitted four heavy wagons, with ox teams and supplies. He purchased two hundred head of cattle and forty work oxen. He engaged seventeen adventurous young men who agreed to drive the oxen and herd the livestock, in exchange for food and the opportunity to go west. Mr. Rose himself procured horses for everyone who needed one, along with some extras. In California, he would use these animals for his horse breeding program.

The supplies Father stockpiled astonished Sallie: five hundred pounds of salt pork and bacon, five hundred pounds of dried hulled corn; barrels of flour, cornmeal, molasses; yeast, vinegar, coffee, sugar, salt, crackers, potatoes, pickles, rice, and beans. Eggs were packed in the flour barrels. There was even some chocolate for treats.

"We'll hunt for meat on the trail," Father explained, "and probably find wild berries, honey, and maybe even some vegetables growing along the way."

Everything they needed to survive for the next five or six months went into the wagons: leather to fix shoes, cloth, needles, thread, pins, and scissors; saws, hammers, axes, nails, string and knives; a complete set of blacksmith's tools; soap, wax for making candles, lanterns and washbowls; rifles and ammunition. Plates, knives, forks, spoons, cups, pots and pans were kept in a special box attached to the back of the wagon for easy access. Father lashed a water barrel to each wagon's side and hung a grease keg from the back axle. By the time things were in order, everyone for miles around knew that Lawrence Rose had spent more than twenty-seven thousand dollars outfitting one of the finest expeditions the state of Iowa had ever known.

Sallie remembered watching Father and Uncle Charles painstakingly going over a final checklist together, making sure of every detail. Then Uncle Charles had put down the list, saying, "You've a right to be proud, Alpha. Your equipment is first-class, your livestock is superior, and you've mustered together the best group of young men I've seen in a long time. If I were going on a wagon train, I'd want you in charge!"

"There's still room for you, Charles." Father smiled.

"No, no," Uncle Charles replied. "Three of my sisters and my only brother have chosen to move west, but Iowa is my home now, and it's going to stay that way. You just take good care of Mary and all those children, hear?"

Looking serious, Father said quietly, "Charles, I'll do my best. And I know you'll help Mary Ann if she needs you."

Sallie sensed that leaving Mary Ann behind was Father's only regret about the journey. A recent bride, she would stay in

Keosauqua with her husband. Father had tried to talk the newlyweds into coming along, but they had decided against it. At first, Liefy had wanted to stay behind too, but despite her protests, Father had insisted she come to California with them.

Father turned away from Uncle Charles and playfully called to Sallie and her sisters, "Who can tell me when this wagon train will be ready to roll?"

"When the grass comes in!" the girls sang out in unison, as they had many times before.

Timing, Father had told them over and over, was as important to the success of the journey as wagons, food, and equipment. If they left too early in the spring, they might bog down in mud, and spend days digging their wagons out of the mire. Also, if they started too soon, there would not be enough grass to feed the cattle. The goal of this expedition, Sallie knew, was to get those cattle to California in the best condition possible.

On the other hand, if they left too late, they might be caught crossing the mountains in a heavy winter snowfall. Folks in Iowa still talked about the Donner Party tragedy of twelve years earlier. Stranded in the mountains by winter snows, many of those travelers had died of cold and hunger. "Timing," Father continued to remind the girls, "is essential."

When Father had gone west in 1849, he'd followed the Oregon Trail, essentially the same route the Donner Party had taken. But with better timing, he had made it over the mountains into California well before the snow fell. For this trip, Father had originally intended to take that route again, across the northern plains to the Rocky Mountains, through Utah, and into California.

But at the last minute, he changed his mind. News reached Iowa of serious Indian attacks against wagon trains in Utah. For safety's sake, Mr. Rose and Father decided to take the southern route, even though it would add five hundred miles to their trip. Thus, when all was ready and the grass was high, it was to the Santa Fe Trail, not the Oregon Trail, that their wagon train headed in mid-April of 1858.

How well Sallie remembered the day they had finally left Keosauqua! The Rose family went first, of course, in their small covered wagon drawn by two mules. Then came the first of the four big wagons, holding Mama, the five children, and the family's personal belongings. Behind them rolled the remaining wagons, laden with supplies. Last, came the livestock, driven by the men on horseback. Father rode his horse up and down the procession, making sure everything was in order.

"He looks like a general inspecting his army," Sallie whispered proudly to Liefy. And it did seem rather like a military parade. Dozens of friends and relatives saw them off, and the children held up the side of the canvas wagon cover to shout "Good-bye Uncle Charles! Good-bye Aunt Rachel! Good-bye, Mary Ann! Good-bye! Good-bye!" until the wagons rounded a bend in the road and their Iowa home disappeared from sight.

When Father halted the train for the evening, they circled the wagons, as usual, and performed their evening chores. Just after supper, they heard a commotion in the distance. Father and the other men raced to the edge of the circle to look. Following close behind them, Sallie peered between two wagons. In the moonlight, she saw another wagon train approaching, about a quarter of a mile away. Father and Mr. Rose mounted their horses and rode over to investigate.

A while later, they returned with happy news. It was a small train consisting of several families from Nodaway County, Missouri, a herd of cows, and eight cattle hands. The train was headed up by two brothers, Gillum and Right Baley. They and their families were joined by the Joel Hedgpeth family, and Joel's married son Thomas, and his family. They had agreed to join the Rose train, although they wanted to keep the two herds of cattle separate.

"This is very fortunate," Father said. "Combined, we'll have a twenty-wagon train with forty armed men."

Sallie was glad Father liked the Baleys and Hedgpeths. He had told her many times how important it was for small wagon trains to band together for safety. But he insisted on choosing his traveling partners carefully. "I'll have nothing to do with a poorly disciplined group," he had declared often. "I've heard tales of wagon trains breaking up into fist fights. Some have split up and completely abandoned each other in the middle of the wilderness."

Sallie knew that before leaving Iowa, Father and Mr. Rose had resolved always to keep control of their own wagon train. Anyone joining them would first have to agree to follow directions as laid down by Alpha Brown. Apparently, these newcomers had agreed to that. Watching Father talking with the others in the light of the camp fire filled Sallie anew with admiration for him. Uncle Charles was right. Father *was* the best person to lead this wagon train!

4. BUFFALO

May 13. Our wagon train now has more than one hundred people. Like a traveling village! I have a new friend, Ellen Baley, who is twelve like me.

The arrival of the newcomers made nooning and evening camp much more lively. Mothers gossiped and laughed as they worked, while the children whooped and hollered, happy to be free from the wagons. Night time brought music, as people reached for fiddles, accordions, and harmonicas. Everyone sang, while the children danced and spun in the flickering firelight, casting happy shadows around the circle.

"This whole trip is more fun now that your family has joined us," Sallie whispered to Ellen. "Even stuffy Mr. Rose seems friendlier." Sallie had never before seen Mr. Rose mingle so jovially with the group around the campfire. Yet tonight he even brought out a guitar. After strumming it gently a few times, he began to sing softly in German.

After finishing the song, he said quietly, "This guitar got me through many lonely nights. I taught myself to play it when

BUFFALO

I was eight years old, crossing the Atlantic on my way to America. It helped me safely over the first ocean I crossed, and will help me over this 'prairie ocean' as well!"

Sallie looked happily around the campfire. Father was deep in discussion with John Udell, a man who had joined their group at the Missouri state line. Mama sat whispering with Ellen's Aunt Nancy. Although Sallie knew better than to ever mention it aloud, Mrs. Baley was obviously expecting a baby. Sallie wondered if it would be born before they reached California. Liefy sat beyond Mama, chatting with Ellen's older sisters.

Sallie was suddenly struck by an odd thought. Liefy, who had always seemed so sickly at home, seemed positively radiant in recent days. She smiled more, spoke more, and her face glowed in a way Sallie had never noticed before. Life on the trail certainly agrees with her, Sallie mused. Who would have guessed?

May 14. We met a wagon train from Santa Fe, carrying goods to sell back home. Father paid the captain to mail letters for us in St. Louis. Mama wrote to Uncle Charles, and Liefy wrote to Mary Ann. Won't they be surprised to hear from us so soon?

As Sallie finished writing that entry in her journal, a tremendous rumbling sound made her jump with surprise. "*What's that?*" she yelped, scrambling to look out the front of the wagon. To the far right, she saw an enormous dust cloud, and a huge brown mass that seemed to bounce along the prairie.

"*Buffalo!*" she and Francie shouted in unison.

Orrin clapped his hands and whooped with delight.

"Fresh meat!" yelled Francie.

"No more Old Ned!" cried Sallie, using the cattle hands' nickname for salt pork.

"Father was right!" Julia cried out. "He said we'd see buffalo soon!"

Sallie stared at the great beasts with their shaggy hair and humped backs. "They're ugly!"

"And so big!" Julia added.

"Father says the biggest ones weigh more than one thousand pounds," Francie said. "But the small ones taste better."

Sallie called to Will Harper, in his usual place driving the oxen, "Are you going to shoot us one of those, Will?"

"I'll shoot two!" Will shouted back. "Just as soon as your papa says I can stop this here wagon!"

Father didn't call a halt till sunset, so Will and the other drivers stalked no buffalo that day. However, the men on horseback were freer to do what they liked. Half-crazed with excitement, they galloped after the buffalo, shooting haphazardly. Some of the bullets met their mark, and a few animals fell dead in the dust. The exuberant young men laughed with delight at their success, and then rode on, leaving the dropped carcasses to bake in the sun and be set upon by wolves and buzzards.

Father disapproved of this wanton destruction. "Save your ammunition for when it counts," he advised the men later. "Tomorrow we'll go on a real hunt. Then we'll see what you can do with a rifle!"

Excitement filled the camp that night, as the men cleaned their firearms and made other preparations. Father had hunted buffalo before, and Sallie knew from his stories what to expect. The carcasses would weigh far too much to be dragged back to camp. Instead, the men must be ready to butcher the fallen animals on the spot, bringing back only the choicest parts: the tongue, the hump-ribs, and the tender-loin.

"What about the skins?" Sallie asked. "Will we soon have a fine buffalo skin rug to sleep on?" She had long admired two plush buffalo rugs belonging to the Rose family, and wanted one for herself.

"I'm afraid not, my dear," laughed Father. "Turning a hairy, smelly buffalo skin into a soft and inviting rug is a long, painstaking process. We won't have time for that. For now, you'll just have to content yourself with a tasty meal."

Fervently wishing they could join in the next day's outing, the children playacted a hunt of their own. Gillum Baley good-naturedly impersonated the buffalo, while the little children stalked him with imaginary rifles. After staggering along for a while, as though wounded, the pretend buffalo noisily collapsed on the ground saying, "Alas, you've shot me. Now the stew pot is my destiny!"

The next morning's cold and rain did not dampen the buffalo hunters' enthusiasm. They left at first light, while the women and children lingered in bed. Later, after everyone was up and had eaten breakfast, Ellen and two of her little cousins came over to play in the wagon with Sallie and Julia. Mama, Liefy, and Francie took their knitting, and went to chat in one of the Baley wagons.

After the rain let up, Sallie poked her head outside the wagon. "It's pretty muddy, but the sky is clearing," she told Ellen. "Let's fetch water from the stream."

Sallie carefully led the way through the mud until they were well away from the wagon. Then she whispered, "I didn't want to say anything in front of the little children, but I think Liefy has a beau!"

"A beau?" Ellen repeated breathlessly. "Who?"

"Frank Emerdick."

"Frank? You mean the cattle hand? What makes you think so?"

Sallie smiled smugly. "Remember how I said Liefy has seemed so happy these last few days? Well, I've been watching her very closely. Every time Frank is around, she acts *different*."

"What do you mean *different*?"

"She blushes and gets all smiley and giggly. She really does!'

Ellen thought about this for a moment. "And what does Frank do?"

"He finds excuses to come around wherever Liefy happens to be."

Reaching the creek, the girls were startled to come upon John Udell, washing clothes. Sallie knew Mr. Udell, the oldest man on the wagon train, used to be a Baptist preacher, but she had never spoken with him. She also knew some of the cattle hands secretly poked fun at him and his pious ways. Though he often wore a stern expression, today he smiled kindly.

"Good morning, young ladies! We three seem to be the only ones out and about our campsite today!"

"You didn't go on the hunt, sir?" Sallie inquired politely. "I thought all the men had left!"

"All but one, my dear," he replied. "As the Good Book says, '*In returning and rest ye shall be saved.*' Today, these old bones preferred to stay in bed on a rainy morning. Besides, I've hunted plenty of buffalo in my day!"

This surprised Sallie. "You've hunted buffalo before?"

"Yes, indeed. Caught my share of 'em, too!" Mr. Udell replied. "I've crossed the plains to California three times, and each time I've brought down one of the 'prairie beeves.'"

"You've been to California *three* times?" She had thought Father an expert for going once!

He nodded. "Three times across the plains by wagon— three times back home again the long way, by boat!"

"And your wife," Sallie asked, "did she go with you three times, too?"

"Ah, no," the old man answered. "This is her first trip. Our two sons live near San Francisco now, and, if the Lord wills it, we shall spend the rest of our days with them."

After he left, Sallie whispered, "He seemed nice enough. I wonder why he's washing clothes."

"Mother says his wife is sick," Ellen replied. "Says she should never have made this trip."

After the sky cleared and the sun came out, Mama had the children do laundry and hang it on lines draped between the wagons. They also emptied, cleaned, and repacked the family wagon. Just as she finished up, Sallie saw Father and Mr. Hedgpeth, mud-covered and blood-spattered, returning with the trophies of their hunt. She ran to meet them.

"Did you get one, Father?" she panted excitedly. "Did you shoot a buffalo?"

"I felled the first one of the day," he replied triumphantly. "We killed five altogether, and an antelope, too!"

"Where are the other men?" Sallie asked.

"Butchering their animals. They'll be back soon."

"Help us out, Sallie," Mr. Hedgpeth said. "Go find my son Joel and the other older children and as many good meat cutting knives as you can rustle up."

Sallie raced from wagon to wagon, recruiting children to help with the buffalo. Soon the camp was alive with activity. Some of the meat went directly into a cook pot, and some was skewered on sticks and roasted over the open fire. But most of it would be dried for jerky. Father and Mr. Hedgpeth showed the children how to cut the meat into long thin strips. Mama and Mrs. Hedgpeth strung up a line over a low fire and hung the strips of meat to dry.

"Jerking meat like this preserves it," Father explained. "We'll now have buffalo meat for many days to come."

The other men drifted back in small groups, bringing more meat to be cut and dried. Finally, the last horseman rode in. It was Thomas Hedgpeth, with a surprise. Trotting along behind his horse, with a rope tied around its neck, was a buffalo calf.

Sallie and all the other children quickly surrounded the small newcomer, eager to see it up close and touch it. "Where did it come from?" Sallie squealed in delight.

"I caught it," said Thomas Hedgpeth. "One of the bigger buffalo we killed must have been its mother. This little fellow didn't even run, he just stood around looking forlorn!"

"There, there, baby," Sallie said, petting the calf on its head. "We'll take care of you."

"Calves taste best!" someone called out. "Let's roast him for supper!"

"Don't you dare!" Sallie cried out in horror. "He's only a baby! You leave him alone!"

Thomas touched Sallie on the shoulder. "Don't worry. Nobody's going to eat this fellow any time soon. He's mine, and I want him to grow up big and fat."

5. THE ARKANSAS RIVER

Before they left the next morning, Sallie watched Thomas
tie a rope around the buffalo calf's neck, and attach it to the back
of his wagon. How lucky the Hedgpeth children were to have
the buffalo calf walking with them the whole way! Returning
to her own wagon, Sallie thought wistfully of the baby animals
born each spring back in Keosauqua. Settling in for the ride, she
asked, "Mama, may we have a pet when we get to California?"

"Why not?" Mama replied. "Julia and Si have horses and
dogs, and their last letter even mentioned rabbits."

The thought of owning a rabbit appealed to Sallie, but for
now, the buffalo calf was the closest thing to a pet on this wagon
train. Later that morning, Sallie begged Mama to let her go back
and check on him.

"Me, too!" Julia cried out. "I want to go, too!"

With Mama's permission, Sallie and Julia worked their
way back until they reached the Hedgpeth family wagon.
There, still trotting behind it, was the baby buffalo, surrounded
by all the Hedgpeth and Baley children. Sallie and Julia fell in

step with Ellen, and the happy group continued along until the wagons came to a halt.

They had reached the Little Arkansas River, a tributary of the main Arkansas. Although the shallow, fast-running creek was only about fifteen feet wide, its banks were steep and miry. "It's too dangerous to take the wagons across like this," Father said. "We'll have to build a suitable crossing point."

The children brought a bucket of water for the calf, and then sat on the ground watching the men use axes, spades, and mattocks to level off the steep bank. Then the men cut branches from nearby willow trees, placed them crisscross on the bank, and covered them with dirt.

When all was ready, they carefully led each wagon, one by one, across this newly-constructed path, through the water, and up the other side. Mr. Rose's mules balked until a few lashes from the whip got them moving again. Everyone made it safely across, including the buffalo calf, splashing through the creek behind the Hedgpeth wagon.

"I think I'll name him Little Arky, in honor of this river," Thomas Hedgpeth told the children.

"Little Arky," Sallie repeated. "I wonder how *little* he'll be when we get to California!"

May 17. Today we reached the sand hills of the Arkansas River. The water tastes good. Father says it started as melted snow high in the Rocky Mountains. Not much else to look at.

The wagons followed the northern bank of the Arkansas for several days. Except for occasional cottonwood trees right at the water's edge, the only vegetation to be seen for miles and miles was cactus and tight-curled buffalo grass.

"I hope California has trees," Sallie said. "I would never want to live in a place so flat and desolate as this." She sighed.

"Remember Uncle Charles' big walnut tree back home?" Francie asked.

Mama looked up from her knitting and laughed. "Sallie got stuck up in that tree when she was about three years old. She climbed right up when no one was looking, and then couldn't get down!"

"That was July fourth when Father was gone to California," Liefy chimed in. "Sallie's skirt caught in a branch, and Mary Ann rescued her!" They chuckled happily at these memories of home, so different from the barren landscape around them.

One morning Sallie spied hundreds of small dirt piles off to one side of the wagon. "That must be a prairie dog town!" she exclaimed in delight. "It looks like a collection of big ant hills, just like Father said it would."

Sallie watched as dozens of squirrel-like animals peeped out at them. A few of the braver ones sat up on their hind legs. After a moment, the creatures started running in different directions, emitting high-pitched yelps. Were they sentinels, alerting the others to danger? Soon hundreds of heads poked out of hundreds of holes, filling the air with loud barking. "The prairie dogs are talking to each other, Orrie," Sallie whispered.

"They don't look much like dogs, Mama," said Julia.

"They're aren't really dogs, sweetheart," her mother replied. "More like big rats."

"But what a loud racket they make!" said Francie. "They *sound* rather like dogs, don't they?"

At campfire that night, Mr. Udell turned to Alpha Brown and said, "On June 22, I will be sixty-three years old. Do you reckon we'll have reached Santa Fe by then?"

"If we keep up this excellent pace, sir, you may celebrate your birthday in that city!" Father replied.

"And *my* birthday, on August 13?" Sallie piped up. "Will we be in California yet?"

"Perhaps we will. I don't know how long the trip from Santa Fe will take us," Father answered.

Being finished with this tedious trip would make the best birthday present, Sallie mused. But knowing Father didn't like to hear complaining, she kept that thought to herself.

THE ARKANSAS RIVER

May 21. We passed a fifty-foot bluff called Pawnee Rock. Amidst all this flatness, it looked like a huge mountain. Father sent Frank Emerdick and Ed Akey ahead to scout it out, to make sure no Indians lay in wait for us. Now we're camped at Pawnee Fork.

At campfire that night, Frank described what he had seen from the top of that ridge. "It was the most amazing sight! To the east I saw all our wagons and the cattle. Far to the west, I saw a huge buffalo herd. It looked like one big black mass extending all the way to the horizon."

"Sounds good!" Mr. Udell remarked. "Should be plenty of buffalo dung when we need it."

"And that will be soon," Father added. "The captain of that eastbound train said the trees here at Pawnee Fork are the last we'll see for three hundred miles."

Sallie knew when the wood was gone, they would cook with dried buffalo droppings, the "prairie fuel." Father said it would be her job to help collect it. The thought made her wrinkle her nose in distaste!

Taking as much wood with them as they could comfortably carry, the group continued along the Arkansas River for several more days. Once, to their alarm, they passed within sight of a small Indian village. Peeking from the wagon, Sallie saw several large circular tents made from animal skins. She also spied some naked children playing outside one of the tents, and horses grazing in the distance.

Though no one spoke, Sallie could feel the tension in the wagon. Mama and Francie held Julia close, while Liefy and Sallie hugged Orrin. Silently, they watched the Indian village for signs of activity. Sallie glanced sideways at the spot in the wagon where Will Harper kept his rifle. Would he need to grab it fast? The men on horseback carried guns. Would they be forced to draw them? Her heart hammered as she held her breath, listening for any sound of danger. But nothing happened. The natives ignored them, and the wagons passed by without incident. Sallie and her family felt relief when the view of the village disappeared behind them, but a sense of wariness remained. Just to be safe, Father posted extra men on watch that night.

May 24. The Santa Fe Trail splits into two branches now. We'll take the desert route to save time. But first we must ford the Arkansas River. Father says it will be the most dangerous crossing of our entire trip.

Though their wagons had crossed many creeks, all of them had been narrow and shallow. The Arkansas River, however, was a half-mile wide. Its swift-running current hid a river bottom filled with sinkholes and quicksand. Wagons could tip over, entangling panicked oxen in their lines.

"But if we drive the cattle across first," Father explained, "their hooves should trample the quicksand under. That will make a firmer footing for the oxen and wagons."

"Won't the cattle get caught in the quicksand?" someone asked.

"The loose animals aren't carrying extra weight and aren't hitched to any lines," Father replied. "If they get caught, they should be able to pull free."

"What about Little Arky?" Sallie asked.

"I'll make sure Little Arky crosses safely, Sallie," Thomas Hedgpeth assured her. "I have big plans for him in California!"

The next morning, Sallie and Francie stood on the river-bank, watching the men drive the cattle into the river. Some of the animals resisted, but eventually, they all reached the other side without mishap.

"Back to the wagon now!" Mama called to them. "It's almost time to go."

The girls scrambled back into their own wagon, just as Father motioned for the Rose vehicle to enter the water. "I'll bet the mules won't like it," Sallie said, watching the men guide the Rose wagon into the racing current. With water reaching almost to the top of its wheels, the wagon inched forward a short distance. Then it came to a complete stop.

"I think you're right," said Francie. "It looks like the mules won't budge."

"I wonder what words Mr. Rose is using to urge them on?" Sallie asked impishly. The others laughed, and even Mama couldn't suppress a smile. Mr. Rose sometimes cursed his animals loudly, to the embarrassment of his wife and the great disapproval of his mother-in-law.

"Well, he must have said something they understood!" Francie said. "They're moving again."

This time, the mules kept going, and after what seemed like a very long while, the Rose wagon safely reached the opposite shore. Father signaled for Will Harper to lead the Brown family wagon across next. As the swift water pounded against the wood and canvas with a furious intensity, Sallie gasped with the realization of how dangerous her situation really was. Orrin clung to her waist in fright. Next to her, Francie and Liefy held hands, while Mama encircled Julia in her arms. No one spoke. When they were about halfway across the river, the wagon suddenly lurched and tipped precariously to the left. Sallie and Orrin slammed against the side of the wagon bed, and Francie and Liefy landed on top of them.

"We've got you!" Frank Emerdick's voice shouted from outside. "Don't panic! We've got you!" It took only a moment for the men to right the wagon.

"Everybody all right in there?" Will Harper called to them.

"We'll be fine," Mama assured him, after the children were settled back in their seats. "Everything is just fine."

The calmness she heard in her mother's voice didn't match the way Sallie felt inside. But she held her chin up and pretended her arms weren't shaking as they gripped Orrin tightly.

When they reached the other side, Sallie jumped out of the wagon, relieved to be on solid ground again. In the midst of all the commotion, Sallie saw Liefy and Frank exchange several long glances. As Frank returned to the river to lead the next wagon across, Sallie smiled inwardly, promising herself to tease Liefy about it later in private.

6. CIMARRON

May 25. Today we leave behind the Arkansas River to head out across the Cimarron Desert. Father says there will be no water for the first sixty miles. He calls it the Jornada. *I think that means "dry journey."*

Sallie pushed as hard as she could against the big wooden water barrel. It would not budge. Then, Francie joined her, and together they rolled the heavy vessel across the sandy river bank to the wagons. There, with big grunts and a strong upward shove, Will Harper and Ed Akey lifted the barrel onto the wagon and lashed it in place. "There!" Will said finally. "This one is ready to go."

The men moved down to the next wagon, where Ellen Baley and her cousins had barrels waiting. Beyond them, the Hedgpeth children rolled more barrels from the river. Sallie knew their wagons would leave as soon as the water was loaded.

"Julia!" she called to her little sister. "Let's get one more drink from the river before we go!"

Julia skipped happily with her, and they dipped their tin cups into the Arkansas and drank heartily. Wiping her mouth with her arm, Julia asked, "Tell me again what *ration* means?"

"It means you must only use a little bit at a time," Sallie answered. "We don't want to run out of water before we find more."

The girls had heard quite a bit about rationing from Father the night before. He had also told them scary stories about the early days of the Santa Fe Trail, when countless travelers had died crossing the *Jornada*. With no trees or other landmarks to guide them, Father explained, travelers could easily lose their way. Lost, without water, scorched by the sun, they either died of thirst or fell prey to wandering bands of Comanche and Kiowa Indians. Even Jedediah Smith, the legendary mountain man who had explored the Great Basin, the Mojave Desert, the Rocky Mountains, and the Columbia River, met his end in the *Jornada*, dying there in 1831.

"But we have an advantage Smith lacked," Father said. "A trail to follow. Wagon ruts." A few years after Smith died, rare torrential rains had drenched the *Jornada* for weeks. Wagons crossing the soggy ground had made marks that later baked in the desert sun to form an indelible trail. "That was twenty-five years ago," Father said, "and I'm told those ruts are as clear as the day they were made. If we ration our water wisely, we should make it through the *Jornada* in three or four days."

Leaving the Arkansas River behind them, the travelers found themselves struggling over rough sand hills nearly devoid of vegetation. To ease the hard pull for the oxen, the children climbed out of the wagon to walk with Mama. Francie carried Orrin on her back, while Sallie and Julia helped Liefy make it through the loose sand. After a few miles, the road flattened out, and the whole family could ride again.

"This isn't so bad," Sallie commented, watching the landscape pass slowly by. "I see some patches of grass, and even a few puddles."

"Must have rained recently," Francie observed. "Lucky for the cattle."

"Lucky for Little Arky, too!" Sallie said. "I was afraid he wouldn't have anything to eat or drink!"

Later, Sallie and Orrin curled up on a pile of blankets and went to sleep. After a while, Sallie awoke with a start and looked out the back of the wagon. She couldn't believe her eyes. There, in the distance, not more than a mile away, she saw a beautiful clear lake! "Father doesn't have to worry about water any more!" Sallie called with excitement. "Look at that!"

Everyone else in the wagon saw it, too.

"A lake, Mama! A lake!" Julia cried.

"It certainly does look like a lake," Mama said cautiously. "But Father said our eyes can play tricks in the desert. I think it's a mirage."

Just then Francie glanced to the other side of the wagon and gasped, "Look there!"

When Sallie turned to follow her sister's gaze, her jaw dropped in amazement. Coming towards them was the figure of a man on horseback. But the horse's legs looked fifteen feet long, and the rider on its back towered fifty feet in the air! Even Will Harper, driving the oxen, stopped to stare, his mouth agape in wonderment. However, as the rider came closer and closer, he appeared to shrink. Finally, at last, there was Frank Emerdick, right in front of them, exactly the size he always was.

That night, Father tried to answer Sallie's questions about the day's strange sightings. "It's a trick of nature," he explained. "It has to do with heat and sunlight. It makes you see things that aren't really there, or makes things that *are* there seem bigger, or closer, or even upside down!"

"Sometimes a coyote looks like a buffalo, or tufts of weeds look like people," Mr. Udell added. "What appears in the distance to be a band of Indians might really be only a pile of dried bones!"

May 25. Today's mirages looked so real! Whatever shall I do if I think I see Indians? Will it be genuine, or only a desert vision?

CIMARRON

By the second day in the Cimarron Desert, they had used up the last of their firewood. "You know what that means," Francie told Sallie and Julia. "You two collect buffalo chips while Mama and I start supper."

"I don't think we have to worry about running out of *this* stuff," Sallie muttered to Julia as they surveyed the mounds of buffalo droppings strewn along the ground.

"Why don't we start with this one?" Julia said, bending to pick up a large pile of dung.

Just as her sister touched it, however, she was startled by something scuttling out from underneath it. Sallie caught only a glimpse of a strange insect with its tail curled up over its head. The creature quickly disappeared down a crack in the dry earth. Julia dropped the buffalo chip with a frightened squeal, and turned to Sallie with a shudder. "What was that?"

"I think it was a scorpion!" Sallie said. "Father warned us about them. They're poisonous!"

"Ugh!" Julia said. "Are they under all the buffalo chips?"

"Wait here!" Sallie ran back to the wagon and retrieved a stick she'd saved from Pawnee Fork. "Let's try this." Using the stick, Sallie poked at another mound of dung. Two big spiders ran out from underneath it. After giving one more poke for good measure, she scooped up the droppings and placed them in Julia's outstretched apron. The girls continued in this fashion, displacing many different kinds of insects and lizards as they worked. They soon returned and emptied their aprons next to the small cooking trench Francie had dug.

Liefy put some chips in the trench, took a lucifer match from a corked bottle, and lit the fire. The fuel ignited quickly and burned hot. Mama put water on to heat, placing two wooden sticks across the top of the pot. "That will keep it from boiling over," she said. "We won't waste even a single drop."

Sallie eyed the water barrel longingly. "Mama, I'm so thirsty!"

Mama poured some water into a cup. "You can each have a few sips now, and more with supper later."

That night, before bed, Mama put a little water into a small basin, and instructed the children to take turns washing their hands and faces with it. Even so, Sallie looked down at her still grimy fingers with a sigh. It would take more than this small effort to get her hands looking decent again!

May 27. No more mirages. We met an eastbound wagon train of military officers with their families. They travel in fine style, with servants! Their cook told Ed Akey that the officers drink wine from crystal goblets and eat supper with silver off china plates. I'm sure the ladies don't spend their time collecting buffalo droppings!

That night, Liefy slipped away from the group. Sallie's sharp eyes picked out the silhouette of Frank Emerdick behind one of the wagons. Sallie watched as the two held hands behind the wagon and whispered briefly. After a while, Liefy rejoined the others as if nothing had happened.

True to Father's prediction, it took only four days to reach Lower Spring, the end of the *Jornada*. To Sallie's relief, they had seen no Indians, and still had a bit of Arkansas River water in their barrels. But their animals suffered terribly. The rain puddles they'd seen on their first day in the desert were long gone, and grass was scarce. The oxen staggered under their yokes, and the cattle showed signs of dehydration. Lower Spring offered drinking water for the people in their troop, but not enough for scores of work animals and hundreds of cattle.

"Little Arky must be *so* thirsty," Sallie said mournfully.

"Can we give him some of *our* water, Mama?" Julia asked.

Mama scowled at her youngest daughter and firmly shook her head. Julia burst into tears, and hung her head sadly. Liefy put a gentle arm around her little sister. "Don't worry, Julia," Liefy whispered. "Father will find water for all the animals."

While the others unhitched the oxen and set up camp, Father led some men up the dry bed of the Cimarron River, next to Lower Spring. They poked the soft ground with sticks, looking for signs of underground moisture. When they found some, they dug holes, striking water about four feet under the river bed. They widened the holes with their shovels, and called for someone to start bringing the oxen down, a few at a time.

Sallie watched Father as he strode purposefully back into camp to talk to Mr. Rose. "The water tastes terrible, Lawrence," she heard him say. "Brackish. Lots of saltpeter. That can't be good for the animals, not to mention the rest of us."

"Is the spring any better than the underground water?" Mr. Rose asked.

Father shook his head.

"The animals are dehydrated. Better brackish water than none at all!" Mr. Rose responded. "Perhaps the next spring will taste better!"

"It's a day's journey to Middle Spring," Father replied quietly, "and who's to say *that* water will be any different?"

For the next several days, the group followed the bed of the Cimarron, reaching Middle Spring, Upper Spring, and Cold Spring. At each place, the travelers filled their water barrels, and washed their faces and hands. Sallie leapt at the chance to clean the grime off her face, but balked at drinking the water. Sometimes it tasted so bad, she spit it out! However, when thirsty enough, she could choke down a few sips.

Sallie could tell Father worried more and more about the animals. The men continued to dig wells in the river bed, but the water they found this way was of very poor quality. One night, she overheard her parents whispering outside the wagon.

"If we don't find decent water soon, the animals won't make it to Santa Fe!" Father said.

"Whatever shall we do, Alpha?"

"Keep going. Keep looking for water," Father replied. "What choice do we have?"

May 30. Today, I was first to spot the Rabbit Ears, a double peaked mountain Father told us to watch for. Father says when we get closer to that mountain, we'll reach a wonderful campsite with plenty of good water.

For the next several days, the twin peaked mountain loomed larger and larger on the horizon, until the wagon train finally reached Rabbit Ears Creek. Though their journey was far from over, the weary group felt the campsite looked like a slice of heaven. It offered lots of water, good grass, and plenty of firewood. As if in celebration, the skies opened up with a driving rainstorm that night.

Father showed the children how to collect rainwater by stringing blankets between the wagons and weighing them down with stones. Sallie stood out in the rain laughing, watching the water cascading into the barrels they placed underneath the blankets. "Fill those barrels!" she shouted to the sky. "I don't ever want to be thirsty again!"

7. ALBUQUERQUE

For the time being, the storm marked the end of their water problems. Rabbit Ears Creek flowed with clear, good-tasting water, and puddles abounded for the livestock. The wagon train lingered an extra day at the site, for both people and animals to recuperate from the previous week's hard travel.

"Father looks happier," Sallie commented to Liefy, as the two washed the breakfast dishes.

"Because the animals are doing so much better," Liefy agreed. "And the people, too."

Sallie looked around to make sure there was no one standing nearby. Then, she turned to Liefy and teased, "You and Frank surely seem to be doing just fine!"

Liefy stared at Sallie in alarm. "Does Mama know?"

Sallie shook her head. "I don't think so!"

"Promise me you won't tell *anyone*, Sallie," Liefy pleaded.

Sallie hesitated. Did Ellen count? She had discussed her suspicions with Ellen on several occasions. Without giving that away, Sallie finally asked, "What are you so worried about?"

"Father would be very angry with Frank if he knew we were keeping company, Sallie," Liefy said earnestly. "He might even make him leave the train at Santa Fe! You know how he is about keeping the cattle hands in line. And how protective he is of me." Liefy paused, and then added, "Mama wouldn't like it either."

Pondering this, Sallie had to agree. Her parents would not be one bit happy about a cattle hand courting their daughter in the middle of the Santa Fe Trail! And because of Liefy's fragile health, Sallie realized, her parents did tend to treat her more like a child than the fully grown woman she had become. Sallie looked soberly at her stepsister's pleading face. "I'll keep your secret, Liefy. I promise." Then she vowed silently, *And I'll make sure Ellen does, too.*

Resuming its journey, the wagon train left the low flat desert behind and started into the mountains. It was a welcome change, since both water and firewood became easier to find. Once more, their caravan took on the air of a festive traveling village. Mr. Udell shot an antelope one afternoon, and triumphantly presented it to Mama to fix for the whole group. Weary of their steady diet of salt-pork and buffalo jerky, Sallie savored this new meat as though it were a royal feast.

The snow-capped Rocky Mountains, now visible in the distance, gave a magical quality to the landscape. As the wagons wound their way through the rugged, hilly country, the children vied to be the first to spot landmarks Father told them to watch for. They knew each one brought them closer to the end of the Santa Fe Trail. First, Round Mound, a beautifully symmetrical round topped cone; then, Point of Rocks, a craggy precipice about thirty miles beyond it. Finally, the last of the trail's great landmarks, a rocky hilltop called Wagon Mound.

Sally saw it first. "There it is!" she cried out. "And Father's right! It looks like a wagon and oxen heading over the hill!"

Two days past Wagon Mound, they reached a pleasant tree-lined valley at the joining of the Mora and Sapello rivers.

Sallie could see a large cattle ranch there, and a big adobe house and store. Dozens of large freight wagons were parked nearby, as small groups of men milled around the entrance to the store.

"This is called *La Junta*," Father told them, "Spanish for 'the junction.' It's New Mexico's equivalent to Council Grove."

Two days later, they entered Las Vegas, the first actual town they'd seen since leaving Missouri. The village included a Catholic church, several stores, a flour mill, and dozens of adobe houses. Sallie watched with interest as a small group of Mexican children and their dogs ran alongside the wagons, laughing and shouting. Their dark skin and eyes seemed exotic to her, and the words they spoke sounded strange and beautiful.

June 17. We have left the Santa Fe Trail, without actually seeing Santa Fe. The men at La Junta told Father we should go directly to Albuquerque, so we are headed there now. It's so good to see trees again!

For several days, they went south along the east bank of the Rio Grande. Sallie gazed with wonder at Mexican villages and Indian pueblos, surrounded by lush vineyards and orchards bursting with apples and peaches. How different it looked from anything she'd ever seen before! They camped about two miles outside of Albuquerque, intending to stay about a week, to rest and re-provision, before continuing to California.

The next day, Father surprised the whole family by sleeping well past sunrise. Mama and the children had already eaten breakfast and emptied out their wagon before he emerged from the tent. When he finally stepped out into the morning sunshine, still rubbing sleep from his eyes, Sallie ran over and hugged him.

"We took extra care not to wake you, Father," she told him. "You deserve the rest!"

Father took out his pocket watch and looked at the time in astonishment. "This is the first time I've slept past four a.m. since leaving Keosauqua!" he said. "Well, I'm pleased to see you've cleaned out the wagon. I need to haul some items to the blacksmith in Albuquerque. Two oxen can pull the empty wagon, and I'll drive it myself."

"Can I go with you, Father?" Sallie asked eagerly. "I want to see Albuquerque!"

"There will be time for that later," he said. "Your mother wants to bathe you children and wash your hair."

Sallie helped Father load the wagon with the things that needed repair. They looked up to see Mr. and Mrs. Udell walking past them towards their own wagon.

"Happy Birthday, Mr. Udell," Father called out. "But, I promised you Santa Fe, and here we are in Albuquerque!"

Acknowledging the greeting with a nod and a smile, the old man replied, "I would have liked to have seen Santa Fe, but I agree with your reasons for passing it by. Albuquerque should prove a much better place for us to prepare for the next leg of our trip. In fact, my wife and I are headed there now. Going over that pass yesterday damaged my left rear wagon wheel. I patched it, but hope to find someone in town to fix it properly."

"I'll probably see you at the blacksmith's," Father said. "I'm taking things in for repair myself."

Later, Father returned from town with an invitation for the whole family to eat supper with a family in Albuquerque. The children happily piled into the wagon. Orrin, freshly scrubbed from head to foot for the first time in weeks, sat giggling on Sallie's lap. Julia sat between Liefy and Francie, who were both braiding her hair.

"Orrie, you smell so good I don't recognize you," Sallie teased.

"Sallie 'mell good, too," Orrin replied, and everyone in the wagon laughed.

"This is heaven!" Sallie happily announced. "To be clean again, with Father driving the wagon."

"It's so much better than having you out on your horse, away from us all day" Julia added. "Let's have Father drive us all the way to California!"

Father chuckled along with the others. "I like this, too. I get lonely out there on my horse by myself all the time."

"Tell us about the people we're going to visit, Father," Sallie called out.

"The man is Charles Owens, and he runs the general store," Father said. "When he found out I am a Freemason, like he is, he invited us for supper tonight."

"What about his family?" Francie asked.

"His wife came here with him from Missouri two years ago. She's one of the few American women in town. They have twin boys about Julia's age. They live in an adobe house near the store."

"I'm ready for a civilized meal on real dishes!" Francie said happily.

"Sitting on chairs in a real house!" Liefy added.

"I've wondered what adobe houses are like on the inside," Mama said. "Now we can find out."

Albuquerque had a Catholic church, surrounded by stores, several blacksmith and carpenter shops, and streets lined with adobe houses. Father pointed out the sights, sharing some of what he'd learned earlier that day. "Believe it or not, Albuquerque is more than one hundred fifty years old," he told them. "But most of the Americans have come in the past eight years, since New Mexico became a U.S. territory."

"What's a territory?" asked Julia.

"It's part of the United States, but not actually a state itself," Father said. "Like Kansas and Nebraska. If enough Americans settle here, maybe New Mexico will become a state, too."

Father pulled the wagon up in front of the general store, and the children jumped out. Mr. Owens greeted them and led them around the block to an adobe house. Mrs. Owens, a smiling young woman, came out to greet them. Two little boys peeked from behind her long blue skirt.

"You are so kind to have us all to your house," Mama said.

"I'm happy my husband invited you," Mrs. Owens replied warmly, showing them into the house. "We always enjoy meeting visitors from back home." She ushered them into a cheerful room with thick whitewashed walls, and woven grass matting on the floor. Pots of bright red geraniums sat on the window sills, and large pieces of brightly colored cloth decorated the walls.

"When my husband told me I'd live in a house made out of mud, I didn't know what to think," Mrs. Owens said. "But, after being in it a while, I've come to love its comfortable warmth in winter, and pleasant coolness in summer."

Sallie eyed the long wooden table covered with a patterned cloth. At each place were a heavy crockery plate, a steel knife, and a fork with a bone handle. There were crockery cups, large crockery serving dishes, and another large pot of red geraniums in the middle.

"You've set such a lovely table, Mrs. Owens," Mama said. "We're so tired of eating off metal plates and drinking from tin cups!"

With everybody seated around the table, Mrs. Owens served up a sumptuous feast. She called the main course "Caldo de Cordero"—lamb stew.

"It's absolutely delicious!" Mama exclaimed. "But unlike any lamb stew I've ever tasted before. What have you put in this?"

"People cook differently around here," Mrs. Owens said modestly, her face beaming with pride. "In addition to lamb, potatoes, and onions, there are many local ingredients: red peppers, juniper berries, and an herb called cilantro. I'm glad you like it."

For dessert, Mrs. Owens spooned up a steaming concoction into little crockery dishes. "*Capirotada*," she said. "You can pour a little cream on top if you like."

"Capira...what?" said Sallie, looking dubiously at the mixture in front of her.

Mr. Owens laughed. "The trappers and mountain men can't pronounce Spanish words very well either, Sallie, so they just call it 'spotted dog.'"

"Spotted dog?" Sallie repeated faintly, with a look of alarm.

"It's not really dog, Sallie," Mrs. Owens said gently, flashing a reproachful look at her husband. "It's bread pudding, but made rather differently than we made it back home. The spots are raisins."

After supper, the Owens twins took Sallie, Julia, and Orrin outside. In moments, a few Mexican children came over to play, too. They knew a little English, and the Owens boys knew some Spanish. But they didn't have to talk much to build a make-believe fort and shoot imaginary arrows. Sallie watched the little ones play, and then wandered over to a shed in the back of the yard. Peeking in, she saw a large brown and white dog suckling four young puppies.

"Sam! Johnny!" she called to the twins. "You didn't tell me you had pets!"

Sam and Johnny came running over. "That's Carmelita," Sam explained. "She just had babies a few weeks ago. You can pick one up if you like."

Sallie selected a roly-poly white one and cuddled him to her chest. "Look at him!" she squealed. "He's so sweet!"

Julia picked up a brown one and Orrin petted one with spots.

"You boys are so lucky to have puppies!" Sallie said. "All we have is a buffalo calf who has grown way too big to play with. They've put him in the herd with the cows now."

Soon, the twins resumed their game of cowboys and Indians, which Sallie found tiresome. She played with the dogs a while longer, and then returned to the house. She found Father and Mr. Owens deep in a discussion of which route the wagon train should take to California.

"Lieutenant Beale's route along the thirty-fifth parallel will save you two hundred miles," Mr. Owens said emphatically. "And you should find more water and grass for your cattle."

"But the road along the Gila River is better traveled," Father countered. "No wagon train has ever taken Beale's route. Beale's only taken it himself once—with camels, no less! And what about Indians?"

Camels? In New Mexico? But Sallie knew better than to interrupt the adults' conversation. She'd ask Liefy about it later.

"There's always a threat of Indian attack, no matter which route you take," Mr. Owens replied. "I say, if you shorten your trip by two hundred miles, you decrease your danger of Indians."

8. THE BEALE WAGON ROAD

Back at camp, Sallie learned that she and her family had not been the only members of their wagon train to dine with Americans in Albuquerque that night. Many others had, too, all hearing stories about the much-admired Lieutenant Beale. The next morning, camp buzzed with talk of the Beale Wagon Road, and whether or not they should follow it to California.

As the men discussed it, Sallie and Ellen sat under a tree with Liefy and Francie, mending clothes. Suddenly, Julia ran up to them. "I don't understand all this talk about camels!"

"Lieutenant Beale is an explorer for the United States government," Liefy answered. "Last year he brought a train of camels through here to see if they were better suited for desert crossings than oxen or mules. He was also scouting a new cross-country wagon route to California."

"What does that have to do with us?" Julia asked.

"The new route would go right through Albuquerque," Ellen responded. "My father says it would turn this small town into an important trading post. People here would get rich!"

Francie looked up from her needle and thread. "What do we care if the people of Albuquerque get rich or not? We ought to take the safest route!"

A sudden thought made Sallie laugh. "Remember the mirages we saw in the Cimarron Desert?" she asked. "If we'd seen camels on the horizon we would have thought we were crazy for sure!"

Later that day, Sallie overheard her parents talking quietly behind the wagon. "What do *you* think of this Beale Road, Alpha?" Mama asked in a worried tone.

"I have my doubts," replied Father. "Everyone calls it the Beale Wagon Road, but it's not a *road* yet. It's just a path Lieutenant Beale traveled last year. There are no maps or guidebooks. Certainly nothing like *Commerce of the Prairies!*"

"What does Mr. Rose think?"

"Lawrence wants to try it. The Cimarron took a heavy toll on our cattle. He fears the animals won't survive an extra two hundred miles through hot desert. I am afraid I agree with him on that."

June 24. We don't see much of Father. He spends many hours in town, finding out all he can about the Beale Wagon Road. At night, the men debate around the campfire.

As Sallie lay in bed, she heard the men's voices, loud and sharp. "I thought everyone had agreed to follow whatever Father and Mr. Rose decided!" she whispered to Francie. "Why do they keep arguing all the time?"

"It's a hard decision," Francie whispered back. "Even Father isn't sure what to do."

Then Sallie heard Mr. Rose's voice rise above the others. "Manuel Savedra, the very man who guided Beale safely to California, lives in Albuquerque," he said. "He will lead us along Beale's route. We'll reach California sooner, and the cattle will be in better shape. It's the obvious choice to me!"

Poking her head out the back of the wagon, Sallie saw the men in the glow of the campfire. To her astonishment, Mr. Udell stood up and shook his fist at Mr. Rose.

"You are a foolish and impudent young man," Udell said curtly. "You show more concern for your precious herd of cattle than for our personal safety!"

Turning to the rest of the group, Udell continued, "The Gila route is old and well-traveled. Of course, there will be dangers, there are always dangers. But you propose to travel nine hundred miles through an altogether savage and mountainous country, all the way without any road, except the dim trail of a few explorers who passed through one time last year with a line of *camels*. And, you propose to undertake this long and dangerous journey in the company of women and helpless children. It's more than foolish, it's preposterous!"

Mr. Udell turned to Father, saying, "Mr. Brown, you've crossed the plains before, as I have. You know the importance of staying with well-traveled pathways. Just as a child once burned learns to fear fire, I learned the hard way to be wary of short cuts. Crossing the plains ten years ago, my companions and I left the beaten path one day, hoping to save time. That foolish decision almost cost us our lives! Indians stole our horses and left us to suffer days without food—and we were just a handful of men. This wagon train has women and young children and five hundred head of cattle. The risk is too great. In God's name, don't do this!"

Mr. Rose answered Mr. Udell with disdain. "Old man, you are the foolish one!" he spat out. "I don't need or want your advice. *I* will decide which way we'll go. You will only decide whether to follow along with us, or take your puny wagon and meager belongings into the desert by yourself!"

Sallie saw Father step between the two men. "Lawrence, Mr. Udell, please! It's not necessary to fight!"

Sallie quickly ducked back inside, as Father took Mr. Rose by the arm and steered him towards the wagon. She could hear every word they said.

"Frankly, Lawrence, I'm inclined to agree with John Udell," Father said in a low, matter-of-fact tone. "The route is tricky and not well-explored. It winds around for hundreds of miles—

up, down, and around hills and mountains and deserts. Who knows how much grass and water we'll find? Who knows what Indians will cross our path?"

"Alpha, you saw how our cattle suffered in the Cimarron Desert!" answered Mr. Rose. "The animals will keel over and drop dead before we finish the Gila Trail—and your nest egg of cash will shrivel up in the desert along with them!"

Sallie caught her breath. They needed that money to start their new life in California! But Father didn't answer.

"If we take the Beale Road, we'll have the same guide Lieutenant Beale had," Mr. Rose continued. "What more could we ask for? Besides, Savedra says the Mojave Indians are a peaceful lot. The Gila trail would take us right into Apache country, Alpha. You've heard the same stories about Apaches that I have—they aren't peaceful at all! Let's stay away from them, and spare our cattle as well."

When all was said and done, Mr. Rose's opinion prevailed. Only John Udell opposed it. Sallie had never seen anyone as angry with each other as those two men. Mama worried aloud that Mr. Udell might leave the group altogether, and Sallie caught glimpses of his wife, sitting in their wagon, crying.

Father spoke privately with Mr. Udell several times, and finally persuaded him to stay. "But I will travel with Mr. Baley's group," the old man declared. "You keep that whippersnapper Rose as far away from me as possible!"

June 26. Mr. Baley's half of the train crossed the Rio Grande by ferryboat today. They took their cattle, including Little Arky, to graze on that side, while we wait here for our guide. Father says I shall see Ellen again in a few days.

Shortly after the Baley wagons left, Liefy asked Sallie to walk along the river bank with her. Together, they watched the churning waters of the Rio Grande thunder past them. Then, Liefy turned to Sallie with a radiant smile.

"I have to tell someone, or I'll burst!" she said breathlessly. "Sallie, Frank has asked me to marry him!"

"Oh, Liefy! I'm so happy for you!" Sallie said. Then she frowned. "Too bad Mr. Udell crossed the river with the Baleys. He's a preacher. He could perform the wedding."

"No, Sallie," Liefy laughed. "Not so fast! We're not telling anyone until we get to California. Father's worried enough with all this business about the Beale Road. I just wanted to let you in on my secret!"

For the next three days, Mama kept all the girls busy preparing for the final leg of their journey to California. All clothes were mended and washed, all bedding aired out. All boxes, barrels, and the wagon itself were emptied, cleaned, and re-packed. Since Sallie had outgrown her leather boots, Father bought her new ones in town.

Sallie was glad the activity kept her mind off Liefy's secret. It was just as well that Ellen was on the other side of the river. Promise or no promise, it would be hard to keep it from her!

When the work was done, Sallie and Julia sat under a tree eating two of the fine peaches Father had brought back from town that day. Finally, Julia said, "Albuquerque's nice. Why don't we just stay here and live near the Owens family? I don't want to get back in that wagon."

Sallie put a loving arm around her little sister. She understood perfectly. The thought of bumping along in that cramped, dusty wagon for another month or more seemed almost more than she could bear, too, even if it would bring them closer to Liefy's wedding day. But she tried to cheer up her little sister. "I think the worst is behind us, Julia. We never have to see that ugly old Cimarron Desert again!"

"Francie says there's *lots* of desert between here and California!" argued Julia.

"But it's different," Sallie insisted. "Father says we'll go through mountains and pine forests, too. And we might reach California before my birthday!"

Finally, three days after the Baley wagons had left, Manuel Savedra rode up on his horse, ready to escort them on their way. He was joined by the Owens family and other prominent citizens from Albuquerque.

"This is a momentous occasion for us, Alpha!" Mr. Owens said to Father. "Your wagon train will help put Albuquerque on the map. We will tell every train that comes through here of your heroic decision. By this time next year, I daresay, the Beale Wagon Road will be the premier route west!"

Then Mrs. Owens and the boys stepped forward with a special surprise—the small white puppy Sallie had admired so much! "His name is Pedro," Mrs. Owens told Sallie. "We want you to have him."

Sallie turned to Mama with beseeching eyes. "Can we keep him, Mama, can we keep him?"

Mama smiled and nodded, taking the pup from Mrs. Owens' arms. "I think Pedro will be just the thing to help these children survive the rest of our trip to California," she said, cuddling the dog and then handing him over to Sallie. With shining eyes, Sallie held him against her chest. "Pedro!" she whispered in delight. "We're so happy to have you!"

Mama embraced Mrs. Owens, saying "Polly, although I've only known you a few days, I already consider you a dear, dear friend! Thank you for everything. I shall miss you."

"My husband always said Masons are like family," Mrs. Owens said, returning Mama's hug. "Who knows what the future holds in store? Perhaps you'll return to Albuquerque some day, or perhaps we shall see you in California."

The Owens family and the others watched from the river bank, as the ferryboat carried Sallie and her family across the mile-wide Rio Grande. After waving good-bye, Sallie turned her attention to Pedro, wriggling in her lap. What a happy turn of events! A wonderful puppy like this would surely liven up otherwise dreary days of travel.

With the wagons safely across, the men returned to help load the cattle into the ferryboat. Sallie spied Ellen and her cousins running to meet them. "Ellen, look!" she shouted. "We have a puppy!"

As the younger children played with Pedro, Liefy and Francie sat nearby. Suddenly, they all heard loud shouts coming from the river. Sallie leapt up and raced to investigate, with the others close at her heels. Sallie was first to reach Mama, her face ashen and her mouth taut. Gently steering the children away from the river's edge, Mama said softly, "There's been an accident. Frank Emerdick is dead."

"*Frank, dead?*" Sallie shrieked. "What happened?"

"Two cows fell into the water, knocking Frank in with them," Mama said. "The swift current pulled him under, and he drowned despite everyone's best efforts to save him."

Sallie spun around and looked at Liefy, who collapsed on the ground with an anguished cry.

"*Relief?*" Mama called in surprise.

Sallie swooped down and enveloped her stepsister in her arms. Liefy clutched at Sallie's neck, sobbing uncontrollably. Looking up at Mama's puzzled face, Sallie hastily explained, "Liefy was in love with Frank! They planned to marry in California!"

Mama stared at Liefy in astonishment. Then, she briskly placed her hands on her stepdaughter's shoulders, and guided her to the shade of a tree. Sallie spread a quilt on the ground, and Mama helped Liefy lie down on it. Cradling her head in her lap, Mama gently stroked her stepdaughter's hair.

A short while later, Mrs. Baley told them people were gathering on the river bank to bury Frank.

"Relief," said Mama. "You must pull yourself together. The wagons will be going soon. We must pay our respects to Frank now."

With Sallie and Mama holding her up, Liefy stood silently by the river as Mr. Udell quietly intoned, "The Lord is my shepherd, I shall not want...." At the conclusion of the prayer, Sallie numbly helped Mama lead Liefy back to the wagon. In a daze, she heard Will Harper crack his whip, and felt the wagon jerk forward. Then, Sallie handed Pedro to Liefy, who clutched the puppy in her arms, wetting his fur with her tears.

9. EL MORRO

For several days, the group followed an established road headed towards Fort Defiance, an American military outpost. Sallie spent much of her time at Liefy's side, offering silent comfort to her grieving stepsister. Sometimes they walked together next to the wagon. But Liefy's leg hurt more these days, and mostly they rode, taking turns holding the puppy. Liefy spoke little, but seemed to appreciate Sallie's presence. When they camped in the evening, Liefy would go to bed while it was still light, and Sallie would sit next to her and sew.

On July fourth, the road they followed forked—on the right to Fort Defiance, and the left to California. As their wagon lumbered to the left, Francie called out, "This is it! We're now officially on the Beale Road!"

At that moment, Sallie brought out a small cloth banner with red and white stripes, and a corner square of blue.

"An American flag!" cried Julia. "Where did you get it?"

"I made it," Sallie said proudly. "Mama gave me scraps of cloth. What's the Fourth of July without a flag?"

"July fourth is not only the birth of our country," Francie said solemnly. "Now it marks the day we become the first emigrant train to embark the Beale Wagon Road!"

Julia and Orrin clapped with glee, begging for the privilege of holding and waving their new banner. The flag was soon forgotten, however, when the wagon began lurching violently. Sallie could see Will Harper struggling with the animals, and then he brought them to a stop.

"Everyone out of the wagon!" he called. "It's too hard on the oxen. We might break the wheels!"

Sallie helped Liefy out of the wagon, and then looked at the ground with astonishment. She had never seen anything like it! Everywhere, crusts of black rock poked up like needles in a pincushion.

"Lava," Mama said. "Father said we'd pass over a volcanic ridge."

Sallie picked up a small piece of the black rock and studied it closely. "This came from a *volcano*?" She turned the lava over in her hand a few times, and slipped it into her pocket. Then, she took Liefy's arm, and the two slowly made their way over the bumpy ridge with the others. Luckily, the ground smoothed out after a while, and became much easier to travel.

July 7. Liefy still seems so sad, and her leg hurts terribly. We are camped at the base of a huge sandstone bluff, which our guide calls El Morro. He says it's the most famous landmark in New Mexico, and that hundreds of travelers have carved their names on it.

"Mama!" Sallie pleaded. "Mr. Rose is going to lead some people up the cliff to look at the names. Ellen's going, and her older sisters, and some of the men. May I go, too, please?"

Mama looked down at Sallie's eager face. "All right," she said. "Just make sure you and Ellen stay close to the adults."

"Thank you, Mama!" Sallie shouted, racing first to the wagon to retrieve something, and then off to join Ellen and the others. As they headed towards the towering cliffs, Ellen whispered, "Did you bring the knife?" Sallie grinned and patted her pocket.

Within minutes they reached the nearly perpendicular face of the huge bluff, and Mr. Rose led them up a path alongside it. Sallie gasped at the magnificent view of the desert below. But in moments, she forgot all about the scenery, totally absorbed in studying the intriguing rock in front of her. Hundreds of names, dates, words, and pictures were carved into it, in both English and Spanish. She saw one dated 1636.

"Somebody wrote this more than two hundred years ago?" Sallie asked in disbelief. "Mr. Rose, I thought *we* were the first wagon train to pass this way!"

"We're the first American wagon train to take the Beale Road, my dear," he answered. "But Savedra says travelers have stopped at this rock for generations. Look here!" He touched the outline of a buffalo. "This was probably drawn by Indians. And these Spanish names over here might have been priests on their way to Zuni Pueblo." Pointing westward, he said, "We'll be at Zuni ourselves in a few days."

Sallie and the others wandered along the path looking at dates and names, fascinated by the strange record in the rock.

"Savedra says Lieutenant Beale carved his name here last year!" Mr. Rose told them. "I want to find it, and put mine right next to it! He said to look for a small cave."

"There's a little cave up there," Sallie said, pointing.

Mr. Rose climbed up and peered inside. "It's here!" he called out. "It says Lieutenant Beale, right here!"

Sallie looked up and watched Mr. Rose carve *L. J. Rose, Iowa*, in the soft sandstone. Then directly beneath it, *July 7, 1858*.

"There," he said. "As the first emigrant on Beale's road, my name shall be joined with his throughout history!"

Sallie walked a bit away from everyone else, and found a smooth spot. Grasping her knife, she carefully pushed its blade along the rock, keeping her letters as even as possible. Finally, she stepped back to view what she had carved. "SARAH FOX," she read aloud with satisfaction. An important historical record like this deserved more than initials, and certainly more than a nickname!

EL MORRO

July 8. We are camped at Fish Spring, near the ruins of an ancient town. Ellen and I explored its crumbling rock walls and found pieces of pottery, still in good condition. Who left them here, and how long ago?

The next day, fifteen miles farther, their wagon train entered another ancient city, but this one still had people living in it. *El Pueblo de Zuni*, Savedra called it.

"It's bigger than Albuquerque," Father told them. "And has an American trading post. It's the last place to purchase supplies before California."

As they approached, Sallie saw well-groomed farm plots planted with corn and melons. Nearby, staked corrals held donkeys and sheep. The two-story adobe houses looked boxy, with large ladders leaning against them. As she gazed at them with interest, Sallie realized that none of the houses had doors on the ground floor. "Look," she cried to her sisters. "They climb on their roofs to get inside their homes!"

Sallie and her family were greeted by Zuni children offering food and drink. The American trader, Ezra Bucknam, also came out to meet Father. Before going off to talk business, Father introduced the family.

"It seems so strange to see an Indian city like this out in the wilderness, Mr. Bucknam," Mama said. "It's not at all what we expected. Have they lived like this for long?"

"The Zuni say their ancestors have lived here for more than a thousand years," he replied. "I don't know if that's true, but the Spanish *padres* found them much like this about two hundred years ago."

He pointed to large adobe ruins across the way. "The *padres* built that church, hoping to convert the Zuni to Catholicism. Now the *padres* are gone and the church is falling apart. But the Zuni remain. Perhaps they *have* been here a thousand years!"

"Do they speak English?" Father asked.

"Not a word. A good many speak Spanish, though, a legacy from the *padres*. I know Spanish, and I've learned some Zuni words as well."

Sallie only half listened as Mr. Bucknam explained that the Zuni sold their surplus crops to American soldiers at Fort Defiance, fifty miles to the north. Instead, she eyed a very unusual looking boy standing a short distance away, watching her. He looked to be about Julia's age, and was dressed like the other Zuni children. But his skin was whiter than her own, and he had luminous white hair and pinkish eyes.

"*Don't stare!*" Francie hissed, jabbing her elbow at Sallie.

Sallie whispered back, "*But he's as white as a tallow candle!*"

Overhearing, Mr. Bucknam said, "That boy is an albino. There are many among the Zuni. They have no coloring in their skin or hair."

"Are they sick?" Sallie asked.

"No, they were just born that way."

Before walking away with Father, Mr. Bucknam showed them where some Zuni women were making bread. "Why don't you watch them?" he asked the children. "They'll be happy to let you look on."

Liefy stayed behind with Mama and Orrin, but Sallie, Francie, and Julia crossed over to where Mr. Bucknam had pointed. The women squatted in a circle, babies tied to their backs with colorful cloths, rubbing ears of corn against a coarse stone. As they worked, Sallie noticed they chewed constantly on what proved to be pieces of wheat. When the wheat reached a certain consistency, the women spat it into a bowl, and chewed another piece. Did they chew wheat the way some men chewed tobacco?

Adding water to the freshly ground cornmeal, the women formed loaves and placed them into large outdoor ovens. As the loaves baked, another woman climbed down a ladder from a nearby house carrying a bowl of sweet mush and a wooden spoon. She handed the bowl to Sallie, motioning for her to eat it. Sallie tasted it, and then turned to her sisters. "This is good! Do you want to try some?"

Julia liked it, too, and the three girls eagerly polished it off. Then the women pulled the bread out of the oven, and handed them each a fragrant chunk of fresh hot bread to carry back to the wagon.

In the hubbub of getting ready to leave, Sallie saw Francie talking to Mr. Bucknam again. Much later, with the wagons underway, and the pueblo far behind them, Francie turned to Sallie. "You know that sweet mush we liked so much? Mr. Bucknam says it's a special Zuni delicacy the women make by chewing wheat!"

Back home in Iowa, Sallie would have gagged at the idea of eating food softened by someone else's spit. Now, after four dirty, rigorous months of life on a wagon train, she just wrinkled her nose and laughed at that peculiar thought.

They continued their way through the strange and difficult land. Sometimes they crossed flat open ground. Other times the men had to chop their way through thick cedar and pine timber, clearing a path for the wagons. Always, the days were hot and water holes hard to find. Once more, Mama rationed the water in the barrels. Señor Savedra rode ahead of the group to scout for water. When he found it, he rode back to them. In this way, the wagons progressed from water hole to water hole, as Lieutenant Beale had the previous year.

July 27. We have reached La Roux Springs, where clear cool water gushes from the ground in the midst of a green valley. After all that hot, ugly desert, I nearly wept at such lush beauty. Father says we'll graze the cattle here for several days, while Savedra scouts ahead.

Sallie lay on her back, enjoying the feel of the long, soft grass, as a hawk circled in the blue above her. The sun felt pleasantly warm on her arms and legs. She turned to Francie, lying next to her, and asked idly, "Who wants to go to California? Let's stay here!"

Francie laughed in agreement. "Good idea, Sallie. Let's build ourselves a little cabin right over there next to the spring."

Sallie giggled at the prospect. "Let's tell Mama that when the railroad comes through, we'll hop the first train to California!"

The sisters giggled some more. It felt so good to be clean again, and to relax in the prettiest place they'd seen since leaving Iowa. Even Liefy, so despondent over Frank, had perked up in these beautiful surroundings. Some of the men had gone hunting, bringing in a deer, two antelope, and several wild turkeys. What a wonderful feast lay in store for them!

Their reverie was interrupted by Orrin and Pedro, who both ran up to Sallie and jumped on top of her. "'No, 'no, 'no!" Orrin sang out in glee, "Eddy bring 'no!"

Perplexed, Sallie asked, "What are you talking about, Orrie?"

Her little brother tugged at her and pointed towards camp, calling "'No, 'no, 'no!"

"Okay, Orrie, we're coming," Sallie said, scrambling to her feet. "We'll see what you're so excited about."

When they walked back to the wagons, they saw Ed Akey and Lee Griffin standing next to a huge mound of snow. "*Snow!*" Sallie cried out to Orrie. "You said 'Eddy bring *snow!*'" Turning to Ed, she said, "Where did it come from?"

He laughed and pointed up. "From the sky."

"Me and Ed climbed the mountain and brought it down on this makeshift stretcher," Lee explained. "Just for fun."

Sallie reached down to gather a frosty handful. Who would have imagined she'd hold *snow* in her hand in the middle of summer? Then, with a devilish grin, she packed it into a snowball and tossed it at Francie. When her sister ducked, it hit Mama squarely on the shoulder. Her eyes narrowing with mock anger, Mama stuffed snow down the back of Sallie's neck. More people joined the happy melee, filling the air with joyful whoops and flying snowballs.

The jolly mood continued into the evening. The women prepared a magnificent meal, and afterwards people gathered around the campfire for singing and stories. Even Liefy joined in the festivities. Sallie and Ellen sang a duet, accompanied by Lee Griffin on the harmonica. Mr. Rose played his guitar, and John Udell recited the Twenty-third Psalm. Eventually the little children's eyes drooped, as the fire's embers receded into darkness. Sallie and Ellen sat together, whispering happily, while the adults talked quietly among themselves.

Finally Joel Hedgpeth spoke up. "I don't understand why Savedra has such trouble finding water. The man blazed this trail with Lieutenant Beale. Doesn't he remember the water holes from last time?"

"The desert changes," Father answered. "Water holes dry up. It depends on the weather and the time of the year."

"He hasn't done such a bad job," Gillum Baley said. "He brought us here, didn't he?"

For the next two days, the travelers continued to drink in the relaxing beauty of La Roux Springs, relishing their fresh supply of meat and the pure cold water gushing from the mountainside. On the third morning, Savedra returned. People quickly gathered to hear his report.

"Bad news," the guide told them. "It's eighty miles to the next water. Your animals will never make it. I think you should stay here until the rainy season."

As Savedra's message sank in, Sallie heard the adults around her murmuring in disbelief. Finally, Mr. Udell spoke. "The rainy season is *months* away! We'll run out of food long before then. The cows can eat grass, but we can't."

"You could eat the cows if you had to." Savedra shrugged. "You have plenty of water here, good grass for your animals, fresh game nearby. Better than dying of thirst in the desert!"

Father stepped forward. "Wait a moment, my friends," he said. "We haven't exhausted our choices yet. Remember the Cimarron Desert? Sometimes we found water by digging holes in a bone-dry riverbed!"

"That's right!" said Ed Akey. "Savedra here looked for visible water. Why don't we try our luck digging for it?"

Five men volunteered to help Ed in the search. Sallie watched them ride off, and then looked around at the green valley. Despite its beauty, she didn't really want to stay there. She wanted to reach California before her birthday.

SALLIE FOX

July 31. Ed found water about fifteen miles to the west. We leave tomorrow morning. I shall always remember this beautiful valley as the first place Liefy smiled since the Rio Grande.

Sallie watched wistfully out the back of the wagon as the green landscape of La Roux Springs receded into the distance. It was soon replaced by drab desert and searing temperatures. After only a few hours on the road, Sallie felt ill from the heat. Her cheeks throbbed, and the infrequent sips of water Mama doled out barely affected her parched throat. She loosened her clothing, and tried to make herself comfortable. When Orrin began whimpering loudly, Sallie cradled his head on her lap and managed to lull him to sleep.

For several days they found barely enough water to keep going. Finally, they reached a deep canyon with a large water hole at the bottom of it. Sallie fetched a bucketful for her family. After drinking quite a bit, she and her sisters dipped cloths in it, which they rubbed all over their faces and arms. Right after supper, Sallie fell into an exhausted sleep.

August 5. We've stayed an extra day to rest and water the animals. The canyon offers wonderful shade from the sun. I have never in my life been so hot as during the past few days. It's hard on poor Pedro . We wet his fur to cool him down.

Sallie dreaded getting back in the wagon the next morning. "Can't we stay here another day?"

"What good would that do us?" Francie asked. "A hundred people and five hundred cows have just about finished off this water hole."

It was true. What had once been a huge pool of water had dwindled to a few muddy puddles. Sallie sighed with discouragement.

"It's not so bad, Sarah," Mama said, placing a hand on Sallie's shoulder. "Before Savedra headed out yesterday, he told Father to expect a good spring in twenty miles. We should make it in a day!"

Mollified by that thought, Sallie climbed into the wagon. Within hours, they were again beset by stifling heat. Sallie comforted herself, thinking, *We'll reach water soon, we'll reach water soon.* But though they covered twenty miles by nightfall, they found no sign of either water or grass.

Finally, Father halted the wagons, saying, "We'll make a dry camp here. Without moonlight, we can't go any farther tonight. At least the animals can rest."

They started off early the next day, and had still found no water by noon. At one point, the wagon lurched heavily, knocking Sallie and Orrin off their balance.

"One of the oxen collapsed!" Francie gasped.

"Everybody out of the wagon!" Will Harper shouted.

Sallie watched Will unhitch the unconscious ox and pour a canteen of water down its throat. In the distance, a horseman rode towards them. "It's Señor Savedra!" Sallie called out. "He's found water!"

But the guide's face was grim as he swung down from his horse. "The spring I expected to find was dried up. It's sixty miles to the next water."

Savedra's devastating news quickly spread from wagon to wagon. Sixty miles! It was too far. The animals had already traveled more than twenty-five miles from their last water, in punishing heat. Another sixty miles without water would kill them for sure.

Sallie watched as Father called together a council of the men, one representative from each family. "The closest water we know about is twenty-five miles behind us, back at the canyon, " Father said. "I think we should turn around and go back to it. If our animals don't get water soon, they'll die. And if they die, *we* die."

"I disagree," Mr. Udell protested. "There wasn't enough water left back there to make it worth turning around. Better to keep pressing towards our goal! We can send out more riders to find water."

The men discussed it for a while. Finally, all but Mr. Udell voted to turn back. Will Harper exchanged the ailing ox for one of the extras, and turned the wagon around.

SALLIE FOX

On the way back, Sallie's family sat in hot silence, as the oxen struggled and strained. Traveling late into the night, they finally reached their old encampment. The animals had now gone more than fifty miles without water. The bottom of the steep canyon was cloaked in darkness. The men stopped the wagons at the top of the canyon and unhitched the animals. The thirst-crazed beasts plunged blindly down the steep canyon path to the waterhole below.

10. MORE TROUBLE

August 8. This morning we moved the wagons back down into the canyon to our old camp. The water is stagnant and full of wigglers.

Though what water remained was scant and of poor quality, the site offered shade, trees, and grass for the animals. The group decided to stay put, while Ed Akey and several others set off on horseback to look for water. Determined to put this forced delay to good use, Father and Mr. Hedgpeth began making extra casks from nearby pine and cedar trees.

"It might have helped us if we'd made these barrels back at La Roux Springs," Sallie complained to Francie. "But what possible good will they do us now?"

Overhearing her remark, Mr. Udell walked over and placed a firm hand on Sallie's shoulder. "It's an act of faith, my dear!" he said. "While we pray to the Lord to bring us water, we must do our part to prepare for it!"

Mr. Udell joined Father and Mr. Hedgpeth, and soon others did, too. Sallie helped for a while, but found it tedious. Wanting to be alone, she climbed a tree and sat there forlornly.

Oh, to be back home in Keosauqua, sitting in the big walnut tree! To draw water from the well, and drink her fill! Hot tears rolled down her cheeks, and she licked at them carefully, not wanting to waste even a drop of moisture.

For several days, Sallie spent most of her time up in that tree, avoiding everyone. She stared at the steep walls of the rocky chasm, which kept sunlight from hitting the canyon floor. Sometimes, she peered straight up, catching glimpses of bright blue through the leaves of the tree. Would this be her last view of the sky, from the bottom of this gloomy desert canyon? When the mosquito-laden puddles dried up, would she dry up with them?

Then, one afternoon, perched in her tree, she saw something that made her heart leap. There, above her, through the leaves! What used to be blue now looked gray and foreboding. She watched with mounting anticipation as the sky grew darker and darker. Suddenly, a tremendous clap of thunder shook the canyon, and rain pelted down with a fierce intensity.

"It's raining, it's raining!" Sallie sang out as she jumped down.

"Bring out everything that can hold water!" Father shouted.

As the rain poured, people sprang into action. Along with the new casks, the men placed out every bucket and barrel. From the supply boxes, the women and children brought out every pot, pan, plate, bowl, and cup. Sallie and Francie hung blankets between the wagons, the way Father had shown them at Rabbit Ears Creek. Tents, pieces of canvas, even the wagon covers themselves, were arranged to collect water. Some of the men even placed their hats upside down to catch rain.

When all this was done, Sallie stood with her arms outstretched and her face to the sky, letting the rain drench her with its delicious wetness. Suddenly she remembered something. "Francie, Julia, Liefy," she called out. "Do you know what day it is? August 13th. *My birthday.*"

August 14. I am thirteen years old, and not thirsty any more! Yesterday's rain lasted only an hour, but our water barrels are full again. To celebrate, my sisters and I sang hymns late into the night. Mama finally told us to hush up and go to sleep.

Sallie tossed a stick across the wet grass. "Fetch, Pedro," she told the dog. "Fetch the stick." The puppy didn't budge.

"You'd have more luck teaching one of Mr. Rose's mules," laughed Francie. "That dog isn't going anywhere."

"Let me try," Julia said, picking up another stick. But before she could throw it, the girls looked up to see Ed Akey and the rest of the search party riding into camp. They had been gone six days. Forgetting the puppy for now, Sallie, Francie, and Julia ran over to where Father and Mr. Rose were greeting the returned men.

"We found a big spring eighty miles ahead," Ed told them. "Nothing closer. But yesterday's storm surely filled up more holes along the way!"

"I agree," Father replied. "Let's head out immediately, to make up for lost time."

For the next several days, the group made good progress in retracing their journey of the previous week. The children, relieved and refreshed by this change in luck, played happily in the wagon with Pedro, singing songs and telling stories. Whenever the men found water, they re-filled their casks. When forced to make a dry camp, they had enough for the animals and themselves.

August 18. Our guide calls this place Peach Tree Springs. I don't know why, since there isn't a peach tree in sight. But there are other trees, and excellent water. Our good fortune continues.

That evening, just before dark, Ed Akey and Lee Griffin spotted Indians in the distance. Sallie's heart pounded when she heard this. *Indians.* She had been so worried about dying from thirst she had forgotten about Indians! Father posted extra guards that night. Sallie slept fitfully, waking with a start at the slightest sound.

The next morning, Father delivered disturbing news. "Two animals are missing," he said. "One of Mr. Rose's mares and Savedra's mule."

Sallie turned cold with fear. Even with extra guards posted, Indians had entered their camp unseen and unheard by anyone. What if they had carried *her* off instead of Savedra's mule? The thought made her sick in the pit of her stomach.

"There's nothing to be done now, but to get on our way as quickly as possible," Father told them. With Savedra riding one of the extra horses, the wagons headed out.

August 19. We have stopped in a little valley with a spring. There are Indians in our camp, talking to Savedra. Mama won't let us out of the wagon. I wish I could talk with Ellen.

After the visitors left, Father came to the wagon to speak to Mama. "They are Cosnino Indians and know some Spanish," he said. "They told Savedra the Mojaves stole our animals, and they took them from the Mojaves. They say they'll bring them back tomorrow."

"Do you believe them?" asked Mama.

"I don't know what to believe," Father replied. "Lawrence promised them a reward for returning the animals. That might be a mistake. We have no choice but to continue as planned and see what happens. Keep the children in the wagon at all times."

Father again posted extra guards, and the travelers passed another tense night. To her dismay, Sallie looked out the next morning to see about thirty Indians riding into camp, bringing the stolen animals. True to his word, Mr. Rose gave them many presents: blankets, shirts, beads, and tobacco. He also served food to the entire group.

As soon as the Indians finished eating and left, the wagon train headed out. The oxen pulling Sallie's family managed to keep going through the day's stifling heat, but one of the Hedgpeth animals fell dead. After fourteen uncomfortable miles, the group reached White Rock Spring, a good water supply deep in a canyon.

After the wagons were circled, Sallie watched from a distance, as Father, Mr. Rose, and Gillum Baley conferred privately for a long time. Eventually, the three men called the whole company together to discuss a new plan.

"Both herds of cattle are suffering terribly from the heat," Father began. "And keeping the two herds separate isolates the men too much. We're going to combine the herds."

"Makes sense," someone said, while others nodded.

"Furthermore," Father continued, "we don't want to drive our weakened cattle without knowing where the next water or grass will be. So the cattle hands and I will keep the herd here for several days to let them recuperate."

This brought murmurs of surprise from the crowd.

"Mr. Rose will lead his half of the wagon train on ahead tomorrow morning," said Father. "Mr. Baley's half will stay here, and follow in another day or two. When Mr. Rose finds enough water and grass for the cattle, he'll send word for us to bring them up."

At that, Mr. Udell strode to the front of the crowd. "*Split the train?*" the old man thundered. "Have you completely lost your wits? Splitting up makes us easier targets!"

"These Indians are annoying, but they have not hurt us," Mr. Rose answered. "In the meantime, our cattle are dropping from thirst and starvation."

"Leave the cattle behind if you must," argued Mr. Udell. "But don't split the wagon train. It's sheer folly. Our large size is our best protection!"

"Even without the cattle, we have more than sixty oxen and mules. The work animals alone would overwhelm a small spring," Mr. Rose countered. "Better to travel in smaller groups, and make better use of the water and grass."

When Sallie realized what they were saying, she blurted loudly, "Leave Father *behind?*" She knew the children were supposed to keep quiet, but she couldn't stop herself. "We can't. We *mustn't!*"

"*Sarah!*" Mama reproved with a harsh whisper. "Hold your tongue or go sit in the wagon this minute!"

Stung by Mama's reproach, Sallie fell silent, but angry tears welled up in her eyes. They couldn't leave Father behind in this wretched desert! What if the Indians attacked, and he wasn't there to protect them? What if something happened to *him* back here without them? She didn't care about the stupid cattle any more. Why didn't they heed Mr. Udell's advice and stay together?

In the end, all the men favored the new plan except Mr. Udell. The next morning, Mr. Rose sat resolutely at the reins of his mules, leading ten of the wagons forth. Sallie sat stoically in the family wagon. Not wanting to break down weeping, she dared not watch out the back of the wagon as Father and the cattle disappeared in the distance. Liefy reached over and firmly grasped Sallie's hand. Sallie clutched at it fiercely, fighting back tears.

August 23. We're camped at Savedra Springs, which Lieutenant Beale named after our guide last year. Oh, happy day! There is so much grass and water, Mr. Rose has sent his wife's brother, Ed Jones, to tell Father to bring the cattle up. Soon we shall be reunited!

Sallie sat in the shade of a tree, mending the frayed hem on her skirt. Mr. Rose strode by impatiently. "Where *is* that boy? I told him to ride straight to Alpha Brown and back! He never *has* been one to follow directions well, now, has he?"

"Lawrence," Amanda Rose said soothingly to her husband. "It's probably a hundred and twenty degrees out. Give the boy a chance! Can you blame Ed for stopping to rest at the spring with Alpha and the others before heading back?"

Sallie finished her mending, and rose to return the needle and thread to Mama's sewing box. Just then, she heard the thunder of galloping hooves. She looked up to see Ed's horse, Picayune, bearing down on the camp at full speed. Startled, she jumped out of the way as Picayune came to a halt next to the first wagon. Ed Jones fell unconscious to the ground, an arrow in his back.

"*Eddy!*" Mrs. Rose shrieked, running to her brother's side. Her parents followed close behind. "Eddy!"

Dumbstruck with horror, Sallie supposed the young man dead. Miraculously, he was not. Mrs. Rose pulled out the arrow, and treated his wounds as best she could. She placed wet cloths on his fevered brow, and tried to make him comfortable. But he was obviously in great pain, fading in and out of consciousness.

As the others worried about whether Ed would live or die, Sallie was beside herself with grief for Father. What if Indians had attacked him, too?

"Perhaps Ed will be able to tell us something in the morning," Mama said. "Until then, we must stay calm and hope for the best. Father wouldn't want us getting ourselves all worked up now, would he?"

Mama's cool demeanor did little to allay Sallie's panic. She and her sisters sobbed themselves to sleep in the wagon that night. At dawn, Sallie woke to the sound of more galloping horse hooves. She looked out to see Father riding into camp, fit as a fiddle!

Mama raced out of her tent. As Father dismounted, she threw herself into his arms, crying out, "I didn't know if you were alive or dead! I feared the savages who shot poor Ed might have ambushed you as well."

"I'm sorry you were so worried, Mary," Father replied, returning her embrace. "Indians did shoot at us during the night. They killed some of the cattle."

August 24. After Father received Ed's message, he and the men drove the herd through the night to get here. He says the Baley wagons are two days behind us. I am so worried about Ellen! Father now says splitting up was a hideous mistake, but it's too dangerous to wait for the Baleys to catch up. We will keep going and pray.

"We shouldn't take this Indian attack lying down," Will Harper told Father. "We've got ammunition and horses. Let's go after those redskins and show them what we're made of!"

"Will, we might kill off a few Indians with our rifles," Father answered. "And then five hundred more will swoop down and exterminate our entire company. Our best chance is to get to the Colorado River as quickly as possible."

Savedra said they were still days away from the river. They headed out into the sweltering heat once more, with most people at the point of nervous exhaustion. Though Mama knitted calmly in the wagon, Sallie recognized the flash of fear in her mother's eyes.

August 27. Liefy and Orrin aren't faring well in the intense heat. Both are pale and weak, complaining of nausea. Savedra says one more mountain ridge stands between us and the Colorado. No sign of Indians today.

At sunset, the wagons reached the top of the ridge. Though everyone was thirsty, footsore, and bone weary, they scrambled out of the wagons to look. There, far below them, Sallie saw the Colorado River, meandering through a green valley. Beyond it lay their goal, California, the dream that had kept them going these past few months.

Sallie lifted up her brother. "Can you see California, Orrie? That's where Uncle George and Aunt Julia live. Right across that river, we will be safe and happy and will never worry about Indians or anything else ever again!"

11. THE COLORADO RIVER

Mr. Rose clapped a friendly hand on Father's shoulder, and pointed to the western horizon. "I predict we'll see San Bernardino in ten days. And when we get there, Alpha, I'll buy you the finest steak dinner you've ever tasted!"

"I'll accept, Lawrence," Father laughed. "I have another prediction. I say we'll reach the banks of the Colorado by midnight tonight."

Sallie hopped back into the wagon with renewed vigor. Even Liefy and Orrin looked a little better. She settled down with Orrin on her lap and Pedro curled beside her. Just as the wagon started moving, however, she stifled a scream. There, behind the wagon, stood four Mojave Indians. Father and Savedra hurried over to talk to them.

"Did they come out of thin air?" Sallie whispered.

"They must have been watching us all along," Francie answered.

Sallie shuddered at the thought. However, the Mojaves seemed friendly. They offered Father two melons and several ears of corn. As Savedra translated, Father gave them tobacco and beads in trade. Though Sallie desperately wished the Indians would leave them alone, they did not. Instead, the Mojaves walked beside the wagons for several hours, and then vanished as quickly as they had appeared.

August 28. We have gone straight through the night and all morning long without stopping, and still have not reached the Colorado. The oxen can barely continue, and Liefy is dizzy from the heat. We fashioned her a pallet to lie on in the wagon.

At lunch time, Mama sliced the two small melons brought by the Indians. "The moisture from the melon will be your drink," she said simply. "The water cask is empty."

Sallie ate slowly, savoring the melons' smooth wetness. Closing her eyes, she pictured the Colorado River snaking between lush green banks. *Soon,* she thought. *We'll be there soon.*

Shortly thereafter, Father halted the train. He rode over to Will Harper and said, "The oxen can't take this any more. They'll die here, practically in sight of the river. Unhitch them. We'll come back for the wagons later." Then, Father turned to the family. "We're a quarter mile from the Colorado," he said. "You should be able to walk it." Then he was off on his horse.

Despite the burning heat, Sallie knew she could walk a quarter mile, especially with a river full of water waiting for her at the other end. But could Liefy?

"I can make it," her stepsister said feebly. "If you help me, I can make it."

Sallie tied Liefy's sunbonnet and helped her out of the wagon. Francie carried Orrin on her back, while Mama and Sallie each supported one of Liefy's arms. Julia carried a small bag with tin cups and an empty water flask, as Pedro followed at her heels. Slowly, carefully, the family inched over the last hot stretch to the river. Every time Liefy stumbled or groaned, Sallie urged her on. "We're almost there!" Sallie kept telling her. "I know you can do it!"

Finally, they reached the Colorado. Sallie and Mama found a shady spot and lowered Liefy to the ground. Then Sallie removed her own hot leather boots and walked barefoot into the river up to her knees. Afraid to venture too far into the swift running water, she sat down where she was, fully clothed, and allowed the water to completely soak her clothing. She splashed her face and drank greedily from cupped hands.

"Don't drink too much!" someone called out to her. "It can make you sick!"

Not knowing how much was too much, Sallie allowed herself a bit more. Then, using her sunbonnet as a scoop, she poured water all over her head, arms, and shoulders. After a little while, she climbed out of the river and collapsed next to Liefy.

All along the shady river bank, the men who had driven the animals lay prostrate in the dirt. Some were delirious from the heat, still shouting commands to imaginary oxen. Others, having drunk too much water, lay on the ground helpless, racked with violent heaves. Sallie shifted her gaze to the far side of the river. "California," she whispered. "It will all be worth it to reach California." Then she closed her eyes and slept.

Sallie stirred briefly at twilight. Next to her, Liefy, Julia, and Francie still slumbered. In the distance, she saw Father and some of the other men bringing the wagons into camp. *Good,* she thought groggily. *Now I can have my diary back.* Someone had placed a canteen next to Liefy. Sallie reached over and drank from it. Then, she lay down again and fell back to sleep.

About midnight, Sallie awoke to the unmistakable crack of a bullwhip, and the fierce cries of drivers forcing along near-dead oxen. It was the men from the Baley train, goading their unhitched animals to the river. In the moonlight, Sallie watched Father leave his tent to meet them. How far back did they leave their wagons? Where was Ellen?

The commotion woke her sisters, too. Mama emerged from the tent, and hurried over to them. "Come, girls," she said. "Get into the wagon and finish your sleep there."

"Mama," Sallie asked. "Where are the Baley wagons?"

"Save questions for the morning, Sarah!" Mama replied. "Go back to sleep!"

Over breakfast, Gillum Baley filled them in on what had happened to the rest of the group. "Those last mountain ridges almost killed our oxen," he said. "We knew if they didn't get water soon, they'd drop dead. We left the women and children with the wagons, and drove the animals through the night to the river. Two died on the way."

"Those poor dears back at the wagons must be so frightened," Mama said sorrowfully. "Stranded in that beastly desert for what could be days!"

"If the oxen had died, we'd have all been stranded much longer than that," Mr. Baley said. "Joel Hedgpeth and John Udell stayed with them. They're both good shots and have a lot of ammunition. I trust our families will be all right."

Right Baley turned to Mama. "Mrs. Brown, you will be pleased to know my wife was delivered of a baby girl the night before we left. We've named her Mary Patience."

After breakfast, Father assessed their situation. "The Baley oxen are in even worse shape than ours. They will need at least two more full days to recuperate, before they can go back for their wagons. In the meantime, we must prepare for crossing the river." The Colorado was not as wide as the Arkansas, he said, but was deeper, with a tricky current. "We can't ford it. We'll have to build rafts for the wagons, and drive the oxen through with the herd."

There was much work to be done. The men would tend animals, repair wagons, locate the best place to cross the river, cut trees, and build rafts. The women and children would prepare food, wash, mend, and repack the wagons. Father hoped to be ready to cross as soon as the others joined them.

Just before noon, as Sallie hauled water from the river, she saw a Mojave chief stride into camp with several warriors. Through Savedra, the chief asked if the group planned to settle there. "Tell him we'll leave as soon as the others arrive," Mr.

Rose told Savedra. Then he presented the chief with blankets, tobacco, and looking-glasses. The chief and his warriors took these gifts and left. Later, another chief and more warriors appeared. Mr. Rose gave them presents, too, and repeated that their group would be moving on soon. That night, Ed Akey reported that some of the cattle had been stolen.

August 29. We are almost to California, but our troubles are far from over. Orrin feels better, but Liefy is quite ill. Mama calls it sunstroke. The days are terribly hot, and these visits from the Indians make everyone quite nervous. I also worry about Ellen and her new baby cousin. Are they safe? Do they have enough water?

"Obviously, we are vastly outnumbered," Father soberly told the group. "If the Indians attack us, we'll defend ourselves, but will ultimately lose. Let's not waste time and energy fretting over what *might* happen. Our best hope is to cross the river as soon as possible. That will take everyone's help."

Heeding Father's advice, Sallie diligently performed every chore asked of her. Mostly, she cared for Liefy, who could not even sit up by herself. Sallie bathed her stepsister's face and wrists with wet cloths and spooned salted water into her mouth.

The group rose early the next day, August 30, to accomplish as much as possible in the coolness of morning. By midday, the stifling heat forced all but the most dedicated to seek refuge in the shade. Father, Lee Griffin, and Ed Akey continued working on the rafts, about a quarter mile downstream from the campsite. But the other men, along with the women and children, relaxed and dozed around camp.

Francie and the little ones played with Pedro under a tree. Liefy and Mama napped nearby. Sallie stood on the big wagon wheel, surveying the whole area. She looked across the river. *Ten days! Father says we'll be back in civilization in ten days.*

Turning away from the river, Sallie gazed east. Everything seemed still, though waves of heat shimmered in the distance. Just then, she saw movement in the chaparral beyond their camp. *What was that?* Her eyes grew wide with fear and her heart pounded. *Indians, lots of them!* She jumped off the wagon wheel, and tried to shout, but no sound came out of her mouth. Then, finding her voice, she screamed: *"The Indians are coming and they will kill us all!"*

In the next second, fierce sounds tore the air. Mojave war whoops mingled with panicked shrieks, as arrows rained down on the camp. Mama dragged Liefy to the wagon, shoving her under it next to Sallie, Julia, and Orrin. Then she and Francie piled up boxes, blankets, barrels, anything within reach, to form a barricade.

Everyone else in camp huddled in or under wagons, too. Those who could reach rifles began firing. Amid the chaos, Thomas Hedgpeth suddenly darted away from the protection of the wagons. He dashed a hundred feet to where his horse stood tethered to a tree. As he brought the unharmed animal safely to the wagon, an arrow hit his left arm.

"What a fool, to risk your life for an animal!" someone hissed as he returned to the barricade.

Pulling the arrow from his arm with a grimace, Thomas replied in a steady voice, "A man might as well be killed as be left in this wild country without a horse."

Sallie and her family cowered in their makeshift shelter. Suddenly, Sallie felt a wet warmth above her waist. Looking down, she saw an arrow protruding from her bleeding flesh. *"Mama,"* she shrieked, *"I am shot!"* Then she fainted.

When she came to, Sallie's head was cradled in Francie's lap. The searing pain in her torso intensified, as Mama pulled out the arrow and wrapped her apron around Sallie's middle as a crude bandage. By now, rifle fire had forced the Indians farther away from the camp, allowing some breathing space. Some of the men hurriedly placed an empty wagon bed sideways against another wagon to make a stronger barricade. Then, the arrows began flying again.

"Where's Father?" Francie whispered.

"Down at the river," Mama whispered back. "He's probably heard the gunfire."

THE COLORADO RIVER

Just then, a horse galloped furiously into the middle of camp. "Mary, where's my gun?" Father shouted, and then toppled to the ground, an arrow piercing his heart. Francie cried out, and clutched Sallie's head tighter. Julia buried her head in Mama's lap. Liefy, squashed almost flat between Orrin and Julia, sobbed into the dirt. Huddled with her five children, arrows flying everywhere, Mama could not go to her dying husband. He lay in the dust as the battle raged on.

Sallie drifted in and out of consciousness. Her left side felt on fire, and any movement sent pain shooting through her anew. "What's all the noise?" she mumbled to Francie, who only stroked her hair, whispering, "Shhhh."

To conserve precious ammunition, the men fired only when they had a good chance of hitting someone. Yet, even so, after two hours, they were almost out of bullets. Though they had killed many Indians, they were still vastly outnumbered.

Then a Mojave chief in war paint and feathered headdress stepped forth in plain view. Gillum Baley raised a rifle and shot him through the chest. Shortly thereafter, the Indians picked up their dead and left. Their tribesmen had already driven the livestock across the river.

For some time after the Indians had gone, the survivors sat in stunned silence. Then, quietly, the children began to whimper. Soon, the entire party sat weeping loudly in a tone of utter despair. Finally, with his bleeding hand wrapped in a torn cloth, Mr. Rose came over to Mama. Slowly, the two of them walked over to Father's fallen body.

For the second time in her thirty-four years, Mama looked down on the dead body of a husband she'd loved dearly. Though no tears flowed, her eyes showed overwhelming sorrow and tenderness. Bending down, she touched her husband's cheek and stroked his hair. Then, she stood up and said resolutely, "We will honor Alpha best by saving the lives of his children. Let us leave this place at once."

Slowly rousing themselves from their shock, the survivors took stock of their situation. One dead, thirteen wounded.

Sallie and Lee Griffin were the most severely hurt. Grandmother Jones's wrist had been shot through with an arrow, Right Baley had a bad wound in the thigh, and Thomas Hedgpeth had been shot twice in one arm and once in the other. The other injuries were more superficial. Ed Jones remained in poor shape from his ordeal of the previous week, and Liefy still suffered from sunstroke.

By chance, the Mojaves had missed a few of their animals. Ed Akey and some others quickly rounded them up. There were six oxen, enough to pull one big wagon. Mr. Rose's mules could pull his smaller one. Out of thirty-seven horses, ten remained. Out of five hundred cows, seventeen remained.

Sallie drifted in and out of consciousness as people debated their next move. Their words seemed to float eerily around her. "We can't stay put," Mr. Rose said bluntly. "What shall we do?"

Each choice seemed hopeless. Continuing to California meant crossing the river, the way the Indians had gone.

"How about following the river downstream to Fort Yuma?" proposed Thomas Hedgpeth.

"That's two hundred miles through the heart of Mojave country," Savedra replied. "I don't advise it."

"Our families are waiting for us with the wagons, ten miles back the way we came," Gillum Baley said. "That's the only direction you'll see me going!"

"We could probably manage that far," Ed Akey agreed. "But what do we do then? It's five hundred miles beyond that to Albuquerque. The trip almost killed us coming this way. Do you honestly think we can make it back?"

There was a long, agonized silence. Then Right Baley spoke. "Remember how anxious the folks in Albuquerque were to have us take the Beale Road? I'll wager they told other wagon trains we went this way. It's a long shot, but we *might* meet somebody that could help us!"

12. RETREAT

Hopeful murmurs spread through the crowd.

"That's right!" someone said. "There's sure to be other wagon trains!"

"Remember Charles Owens, the storekeeper?" asked another. "He said he'd tell every train he saw that we took the Beale Road."

"The Mojaves might be heading back for us right now," Gillum Baley declared. "We must leave immediately."

"Right after we pay our respects to Alpha Brown," Mr. Rose reminded them soberly.

Sallie lay on the ground as several men wrapped Father's body in a blanket and weighed it down with a chain. People gathered at the river's edge while someone recited a prayer. Sallie lost consciousness again as the body of the only father she'd ever known sank from sight.

She became dimly aware of a blur of movement around her. As the men hitched the animals to the wagons, the women tended to the wounded, and salvaged a few personal items. Mr.

Rose handed Mama an empty flour sack. "Take what you can, Mrs. Brown. We'll try to fit it in."

Mama gathered a few tin cups and plates, a knife and some forks, a hairbrush and two quilts. Spying Father's gold watch, she picked it up and slipped it in her apron pocket. Then it was time to leave.

Sallie, Liefy, and Ed Jones were placed lying down in the big wagon, on folded blankets. Francie and Julia sat in the back, nearest Sallie. Grandmother Jones and the two little Rose girls crowded in front, next to Ed. There was room for a water cask and Mama's flour sack—no more. Grandfather Jones, too lame to walk, sat in front of the smaller wagon, driving the mules. Lee Griffin, very weak from loss of blood, lay in back, surrounded by what supplies, food, and water kegs could fit.

Will Harper helped Mama mount Father's horse, and handed Orrin up to her. Despite the heat, she insisted Will drape a buffalo robe around her as a shield against arrows. The remaining horses carried Mrs. Rose and some of the wounded men. Everyone else would walk. As the wagon prepared to leave, Sallie suddenly called out weakly, "Francie! Where's Pedro? We can't leave him behind!"

Francie leapt out and found the dog cowering behind some abandoned boxes. She scooped him up and ran back to the wagon. "I have him!" Though it hurt to move her arm, Sallie reached out a finger to touch the dog's fur.

Sallie's body burned with fever, and each jolt of the wagon produced new pain. As Sallie writhed in agony, Francie spooned water into her sister's mouth. Liefy, overcome with grief and her own illness, lay silently next to her. Julia, in a daze, stared stonily off in the distance.

The ragged caravan moved with a painful slowness. As they inched along, the bright hot afternoon gradually faded into twilight, eventually becoming a night so black they could not see their way. "We'll have to stop here," Mr. Rose said quietly, "and wait for the moon to rise."

"How far have we come?" someone whispered.

"About three miles."

Three miles! Even in Sallie's semi-conscious state, she knew three miles wasn't far enough. Indians on horseback could cover that distance in almost no time at all. Her heart pounded, and despite her pain, she clung to Francie's hand with all her might.

Not daring to make a light, the group huddled silently in the dark, ears alert for any sound of approaching danger. Once, an ox shifted its weight, causing its wooden yoke to creak sharply. Instantly, every man reached for his gun. Finally, about midnight, the moon came up and the party resumed its tedious grind.

They plodded on, as daylight returned and temperatures rose. Barring Indian attack, Mr. Rose speculated they could reach the Baley wagons by evening. But what would they find? Would the others be dead? Would their wagons be plundered? Thomas Hedgpeth, astride the horse he'd risked his life for the day before, rode on ahead to find his family, and the answers to those questions.

Despite the heat and their physical distress, the survivors strove to put as much distance as possible between themselves and the Colorado River. They pushed on, resting only when absolutely necessary. At first, the group stayed close together. But, as the day wore on, Grandfather Jones's wagon fell farther and farther behind.

By evening, the rest of the party reached the Baley wagons. To their relief, their friends and loved ones were unharmed, welcoming them with open arms and a well-cooked meal. Alerted to her plight by Thomas Hedgpeth, Ellen had prepared a special bed with a mattress for Sallie. She helped the others lay Sallie in it, and brought her water in a tin cup. Then Ellen spooned water into Sallie's mouth the way Francie showed her.

"How much water do you folks have?" Francie whispered to Ellen.

"Not too much," Ellen replied matter-of-factly. "Mr. Hedgpeth and one of his sons found a small spring a few miles away, and carried some back for us today."

Just as people prepared to eat, Grandfather Jones staggered into camp on foot. Mr. Rose leapt up and ran to his father-in-law, who collapsed on the ground, too winded to talk.

"What happened, old man?" Mr. Rose shouted into Grandfather's good ear. "Where are the mules?"

Ed Akey limped over. "Where's Lee Griffin?"

Mrs. Rose ran to her father, bending over him. "Did the Indians attack, Father? Are you hurt?"

Grandfather struggled for his breath, gasping, "The mules wouldn't budge. I hit 'em and I cussed 'em, and they wouldn't budge. They wanted water. They needed water."

"So what happened, old man?"

"I unhitched them and let them go," Grandfather mumbled wearily. "I reckoned they'd be better off foraging for water by themselves. And then I walked here."

Mr. Rose gaped at his father-in-law with disbelief. *"You let the mules go?"* he shouted. "You let them *go*? We are stranded in the desert on the brink of death, and God Himself gives you two mules to pull your wagon and you let them go? *Foolish old man!* I can't even bear to look at you!" Mr. Rose stormed off, leaving Grandfather lying on the ground.

Mrs. Rose helped her father to his feet. "Leave him alone," she said curtly to the rest of the group. "What's done is done."

"It ain't done *yet*," Ed Akey said. "Where in blazes is Lee Griffin? Did you leave him in the wagon?"

Grandfather Jones nodded silently. Without taking even a bite of the dinner that awaited him, Ed limped back along the trail by moonlight to find his friend.

Sallie slept fitfully. Twice she woke screaming from bad dreams. Mama came to her instantly. "Snakes were falling from the sky, Mama," she whimpered. "One bit me in the stomach!"

"There are no snakes here, Sallie," Mama soothed. "Go back to sleep."

In the morning, as Ellen brought breakfast to Sallie, Ed Akey hobbled into camp, half carrying Lee Griffin. The two collapsed on the ground in pain and exhaustion. It had taken them all night to travel one mile.

The adults held a council to discuss their situation. Although the ten Baley wagons were loaded with supplies, there were no animals to pull them. One hundred people now had only one wagon to carry their wounded, food, and equipment.

The night's ordeal had almost finished off Lee Griffin. To make room for him in the big wagon, Francie and Julia would now walk. Pedro would also be forced to make his own way. Mrs. Rose relinquished her horse to her ailing father. Mr. Udell had one decrepit pony that had not been sent along to the river with the other animals. His wife would ride this while it lived, which the old man feared would not be long. Everyone else would walk, even Ellen's Aunt Nancy, her newborn baby tied to her body with a cloth sling. There was no other way.

Mr. Udell approached Mama, as she and Orrin prepared to mount their horse. "Mrs. Brown, I wish to offer my condolences," he said softly. "Your husband was a good man, much admired by all. How I wish events had turned out differently! But might I say, despite these severe trials, I still trust that the Lord will see us through. I invite you to trust in God, too, dear lady. If it is His will, we will be delivered from our afflictions."

"Thank you, Mr. Udell," Mama replied quietly. "I also trust in the Lord. I find I have no other choice."

Sallie was only vaguely aware of the arduous march the group had undertaken. The jolting of the wagon made it hard for her to sleep, and the heat was unbearable. Sometimes at rest stops, Francie climbed into the wagon to give Sallie and Liefy some water. Occasionally, before she dropped back to the ground in fatigue, Francie put Pedro in the wagon with Sallie. Despite the heat of his body, Sallie took comfort from the feel of him next to her. When it was time to leave, Pedro was again banished to the ground.

Those on foot had an extremely difficult time. After the rocky terrain ripped their shoes to shreds, they walked in bare feet. The sand burned like fire in midday, making travel impossible. Instead, people rested as best they could, in whatever shade they could find. When night brought respite, they trudged on once more. They spoke little among themselves, overwrought by heat, thirst, fear, and sorrow.

Even in the cool of night, no one could go far or fast. They stopped often to rest, falling in their tracks to sleep. One night, Sallie heard Ellen's mother shouting at the top of her lungs. "Stop the wagon! Stop the wagon! *I can't find Ellen!*"

The wagon halted, and Gillum Baley hastily counted heads. Only Ellen was missing. "Who saw her last?" he pleaded. "Who remembers seeing Ellen tonight?"

"She slept next to me at our last stop," said Francie. "Maybe she didn't wake up when the wagon left."

The thought of Ellen alone far behind them in the night struck terror in Sallie's heart. She clutched Liefy's hand in the dark of the wagon, afraid even to speak. Sallie heard Mrs. Baley weeping uncontrollably.

"Stay here," Gillum Baley shouted. "George and I will find her. Please, everyone, stay here!"

The women embraced Ellen's mother, as her father and brother ran back into the blackness. Tears streamed from Sallie's eyes as she strained her ears for some sound beyond Mrs. Baley's anguished cries. After what seemed like a lifetime, Sallie finally heard Mr. Baley's voice in the distance. "We've found her, Mother! We'll be with you soon!"

Despite her burning pain, Sallie pulled herself over to the side of the wagon and peeked through a slit. There, in the moonlit distance, three figures moved towards the wagon. Soon, Ellen fell into her mother's arms, crying hysterically.

"She woke up and tried to follow us. But she went the wrong way. Praise God, she didn't get far!"

RETREAT

With the three Baleys safely back, the survivors continued on their halting way. Now terrified of being left behind, Julia clung frantically to Francie's skirt. At each rest stop, Mama and Francie slept between the wagon wheels, fingers curled around the spokes. Julia and Orrin would lie between them. There was no way for the wagon to leave without them. Despite this precaution, every time Sallie felt the wagon begin to move, she worried someone would be left behind.

They toiled this tortuous way for three days. Each time a cow dropped dead, the men salvaged what paltry meat remained on its bones. When even this meager supply ran out, they had no food and no water. Sallie's whole body ached, and she could barely even groan through her swollen and cracked lips. Her tongue felt bigger too, as it constantly searched about in her cheeks for moisture it never found. She didn't care about food. All she could think about was water. What sweet, cold water she used to draw from their well at home! Oh, for just one cup, only one cup, from that well!

By now, Sallie knew Pedro didn't have long to live. His dry tongue hung from his mouth, and his body barely moved. One afternoon, the dog's labored breathing stopped. Sallie watched forlornly out the back of the wagon, as Francie placed him in a hole and covered it up. Poor Pedro! He had been such a comfort to her! A dry sob welled up in her throat, but there was no moisture left to form tears in her eyes.

The desert horizon played tricks on them, sometimes showing a broad, beautiful river shining in the sun. The tantalizing image drove some of the thirst-crazed people over the edge of sanity. One man cut his hand to moisten his mouth with his own blood. Just when it seemed the group could go not even one step farther, something appeared that was not a mirage. It was a real live wagon train heading towards them.

"The Lord *has* provided, Emily," Mr. Udell murmured to his wife when he spotted the wagons. "As I knew He would."

The suffering people could hardly believe it when they discovered the wagon train hailed from Van Buren County,

Iowa. Its owner, Bradford Caves, had known Mr. Rose for years. "When we reached Albuquerque, everyone told us you'd taken the Beale Road," Mr. Caves said. "We followed it eagerly, hoping to catch up with you."

But the Beale Road had also spelled trouble for the Caves train. They had started out with plenty of wagons and supplies for their five families, thirty extra men, and one hundred head of cattle. But heat and dehydration had killed off two-thirds of their oxen and much of their herd. Forced to abandon most of their wagons and supplies the previous week, they were themselves suffering from the ill effects of heat and meager food. "We don't have much to share, but we'll do what we can," Mr. Caves offered.

After hearing what happened at the Colorado, the newcomers decided to turn around and accompany them back to Albuquerque. "Let's stay an extra day here," Mr. Caves said, "to help get you folks into traveling shape."

Julia climbed up into the wagon. "Look, Sallie," she said, lifting up her foot. "Mr. Caves made me cowhide sandals. He made some for Francie, too." Sallie eyed the makeshift shoe her sister held up. It was tied to her foot Indian style, with a thong between the toes and around her ankle. She winced to see the crusty, blistered skin on Julia's foot.

Mama brought a canteen and gave each of them a sip of water. "They don't have much water for their own group, but Mrs. Caves gave me this for you girls," she said. "There should be a bit of meat later."

When it was once more time to set off across the torrid desert, one of the already over-burdened Caves wagons found a seat for one more passenger. The ailing Mrs. Udell took it, and her husband rode the pony. Everyone else continued on foot as before.

They still traveled mostly at night, since mid-day temperatures were beyond endurance. The water holes they remembered from their first trip through had dried up. One evening,

RETREAT

Mama's horse fell dead, and after that she walked. She squeezed Orrin into one of the Caves wagons, where the two-year-old lay semi-conscious from heat prostration. Mama walked alongside to stay near him. Mrs. Caves finally gave Mama two knitting needles and a small ball of wool. Mama knitted as she walked. When she came to the end of the yarn, she unraveled it completely and began furiously knitting again.

13. A RAY OF HOPE

The days and nights blended together, as the suffering travelers somehow kept moving. Through her misery, Sallie knew finding water was the group's only goal. Sometimes their search brought modest rewards: a foul puddle in a canyon, a tiny spring beneath some rocks, a patch of grass for the oxen. If water was found, Francie would bring Sallie and Liefy their paltry allotment, usually barely a mouthful for each.

The rest of the time, Sallie lay as still as she could, since shifting in any direction sent stabs of pain through her body. Her dry mouth ached, her lips cracked, and her head throbbed with a desperate intensity. Sometimes Sallie distracted herself by talking quietly with Liefy, lying next to her. But other times, her equally suffering stepsister faded from consciousness, leaving Sallie alone with her pain and her thoughts.

Mostly she thought about water, and how much she wanted to drink it, bathe in it, and lie down and sleep in it. Sometimes, however, especially after the cooling relief of nightfall, she reached for memories of happier times back home—the birth of her baby brother, days in Keosauqua's one-room school house, her family singing in front of their fireplace. But remembering good times brought back images of Father, which tore fresh holes in her heart. As her mind screamed for him not to abandon her, dry sobs sometimes burst forth from her throat. If Liefy heard them, she would reach out a clumsy hand to Sallie in comfort. "I miss him, too," she would murmur. "But you know what he'd say, don't you, Sallie? *Don't give up hope! Patience and perseverance.*"

Two weeks after the Mojave attack, they reached White Rock Spring. They had come sixty miles from the Colorado. Albuquerque was still more than four hundred miles away.

White Rock Spring, at the bottom of a steep canyon, offered more water than they had seen since leaving the river. Those strong enough to reach it brought some back for the others. Julia climbed into the wagon with a canteen for Sallie and Liefy, telling them, "You can drink as much as you like. There's plenty!" Then she burst into tears. "Don't you remember? There was so much water here, we left Father behind with the cattle! And that's when all our problems began!"

Could it have been only three weeks before? How life had changed in such a brief time! Sallie winced in pain, as Julia flung herself next to her, sobbing inconsolably. *"We should have been able to save him!"*

Sallie had no way to comfort her little sister. Their food had run out two days before, and everyone was sick, weak, and overcome with despair. What hopefulness had sprung forth upon meeting the Caves train had long since evaporated. The newcomers' situation was now as dire as their own. Even this good supply of water would not be enough to save them. Sallie felt certain they would all die together soon.

After a while, Mama and Francie came to the wagon. "There's some shade over by the trees," Mama said gently. "Let's get Sallie and Liefy out of the wagon for a change."

With Francie and Julia's help, Mama lifted Sallie out and carried her to the tree. Then they returned for Liefy. While

Sallie's torso still hurt terribly, it felt good to be out of the wagon. She thought back to another canyon a month before, when she had sat in a tree convinced she would die. On that day, her birthday, a rainstorm had saved them. Could it happen again? She squinted up at the sky, seeing only the clearest blue. Not even a wisp of white appeared to feed her hopes.

"Can you give me a little more water, Francie?" As her sister helped her drink, something in the dim distance caught Sallie's eye. "Francie, Julia, look there! What's moving down the canyon wall?"

"I don't see anything," said Julia.

Sallie tried to point, but it hurt too much to move her arm. "It looks like a line of sunbonnets walking over the horizon."

Francie looked hard at the other side of the canyon, and then jumped up in excitement. "Those aren't sunbonnets, Sallie. *They're covered wagons!* Wagons, everyone! *Wagons!*"

Word spread quickly throughout camp, and everyone watched as the "sunbonnets" grew nearer. Those in the approaching wagon train apparently saw them, too, and sent out a rider to greet them. The horse stopped right in front of Mama, who stood at the edge of the group. A man dismounted and tipped his hat to her, showing a balding head.

"Afternoon, Ma'am. E.O. Smith, at your service!"

People crowded desperately around Mr. Smith, blurting out their sad tale. After a few minutes, he raised his arms for quiet. "Wait! I'll hear the details later. First, let's get you folks something to eat!"

Soon, the camp came alive, as Mr. Smith and his men built fires, prepared food, and set up extra tents for shade. To Sallie, the dusty, bearded men performing these tasks seemed to be angels, and their tall, balding leader looked like God Himself!

Francie helped Sallie eat from a plate of beans and crackers someone handed them. Nearby, Gillum Baley and Mr. Rose explained what had happened since that fateful day at the Colorado River. "If you value your life, friends, don't take that route," Mr. Baley advised. "You won't live to see California!"

A RAY OF HOPE

After speaking with his men privately, Mr. Smith came back to the others and said, "We have voted to turn around and join you in your return to Albuquerque. We'll share what we have to help you get there!"

The survivors sent up a cheer, and many wept with joy. Sallie looked over and saw Mama, standing apart from the group, staring vacantly out in the distance.

Mr. Smith's wagon train seemed like a sultan's treasure to Sallie: twelve ox-drawn wagons, forty-three men, four hundred head of cattle, and a good supply of horses. There were no women or children. The men of the Smith train agreed to ride their horses, freeing up space in the wagons. For the first time since the attack, none of the survivors had to walk.

Mr. Smith let Mama and her five children use his own personal wagon. His men made comfortable pallets for Sallie, Liefy, and Orrin and folded blankets for the others to sit on. "Thank you, Mr. Smith," Mama said quietly. "It means so much to have my family riding together again."

As their wagon got underway, Sallie whispered to Liefy, "It's almost like before. It's as though Father is still with us, riding his horse ahead of the train."

Liefy looked away and shook her head sadly. "No," she murmured faintly. "It's not the same."

Under Mr. Smith's care, Sallie felt stronger every day. Though she still had to lie down when the wagon moved, she could sit up for a while at rest breaks. Liefy and Orrin improved as well. Even Mama, though she didn't smile or talk much, seemed more hopeful. Intense heat still prevented daytime travel. However, Sallie found Mr. Smith's cheerful presence made even the long tedious stops easier to bear.

Mr. Smith liked to hold Orrin on his lap, entertaining them all with stories about his wife and children back home in Illinois, and about his previous trips driving cattle to California. One day, he even taught the children some of the Spanish phrases he'd learned during his travels. When food was ready,

Orrin loved to call out to his new friend, "Smiffy, come to beans!" Then, Mr. Smith would hold out a finger for Orrin to grasp, and the two would find a place to sit and eat. Observing this all, Sallie felt confident their new leader would care for them well, and help them safely reach Albuquerque.

One day, as Mr. Smith sat in the shade of the wagon, writing in a small book, Sallie asked timidly, "Is that a journal you have there, sir?"

He looked up and smiled. "Why, yes, it is, Sallie. I try to write in it every day."

Sallie sighed. "Aunt Rachel gave me a diary when we left Keosauqua. I wrote every day, too, until it was left at the river."

Mr. Smith walked over to one of the wagons and rifled through a box. Then, he handed Sallie a book and a pencil. "That's probably not as pretty as the one your Aunt Rachel gave you, but you can have it."

Sept. 14. I dedicate this new diary to Mr. Smith, who has saved my life! With his help we shall cross over this impossibly hot desert, and return to civilization.

However, despite Sallie's optimism, the heat continued to take a severe toll on both people and animals, and water was scarcer than ever. Also, while the Smith train had been well-supplied for a group of forty-three, it now supported almost two hundred people. With the extra mouths to feed, Smith's own provisions soon ran out. Then, he ordered his men to begin butchering the cattle.

By September 20, it became clear that even if they slaughtered the entire herd, they would run out of food long before reaching Albuquerque. Ed Akey approached Mr. Smith with a plan. "Smitty, I'll take twenty men with me and head due south. Savedra says that'll join us up to the south mail road. If we're lucky, we'll meet someone who can help us."

Mr. Smith considered Ed's suggestion. "That's a serious risk. You could be attacked by Indians, you don't know where the water holes are, you could lose your way and die of thirst before the week is done."

"All due respect, sir, how's that different from my current situation? I'd rather die trying to help, than just sit around waiting for the inevitable."

Mr. Smith nodded. "Let's jerk some beef for you boys to take along. Savedra can point you in the right direction."

The meat dried quickly, and twenty-one men prepared to head out across the desert. A lump welled up in Sallie's throat as she watched Ed Akey say good-bye to Lee Griffin. Lee bit his quivering bottom lip, and whispered, "If it weren't for you, Ed, I'd be a pile of bleached bones back there in the desert!"

"You may still get your chance, my friend!" Ed laughed ruefully. Then, clasping a hand on the other man's shoulder, Ed said soberly, "Lee, I aim to get both me and you out of here alive! Someday, we'll drink whisky together, and tell our grandchildren stories about the desert!" Then, mounting his horse, Ed rode off in the moonlight with the others.

Sept. 24. Three oxen dropped dead from the heat, and our train was forced to abandon another wagon. Mr. Smith continues to sacrifice his cows for us, but the meat tastes bad. Today, at least, we have some water.

Sallie lay on her pallet peering out the back of the wagon into the night. Suddenly she saw a brilliant streak across the star-filled sky. She heard gasps from the others.

"Look there!" said Francie.

"A comet!" said Liefy.

"I've never seen anything like it!" Sallie whispered to Julia. Her little sister didn't answer. "Julia?" Sallie asked. "Julia, what's the matter?"

Julia huddled on the floor of the wagon, whimpering, refusing to look up. Finally, shaking all over, she cried, "It's a monster! It killed Father. *It will kill us all.*"

"I don't think so!" Sallie whispered. "I think it's a sign from heaven. I think it means help will arrive very soon."

Sept. 29. We've reached a spring with a fair amount of water. Mr. Smith says we'll stay here a few days to refresh the animals. We eat only bits of boiled beef. No salt.

As Sallie napped in the shade of the wagon, the sound of horses startled her awake. She looked up to see Ed Akey and two other men straggling into camp, their faces thin and wan. Mrs. Hedgpeth brought them a bucket of water, and they all drank greedily. Then Ed recounted their story.

When they had set off ten days earlier, Ed told them, all twenty-one men had agreed to stick together. But after finding no water for several days, they became so thirst-crazed they could go no further. "We split up to look for water, and agreed to meet back at that spot," he said. "The three of us went east, and found a water hole so foul we could smell it before we saw it. It was crawling with little white worms, the most putrid stuff I'd ever seen!"

"What did you do?" asked Lee Griffin.

"I strained it with my bandana, and drank it up!" Ed threw his head back and laughed. *"Best water I ever tasted."*

After recuperating by that smelly water hole for several hours, the three had gone back to the agreed-upon meeting place. They found no sign of anyone else. Fearing the others had perished, Ed and his companions headed back to find the Smith train. "We hoped against hope they'd be here waiting for us," he said sadly.

Ed's story filled Sallie's heart with dread. Though she was thankful he was alive, her dream that he would save them was now dashed. Dared she hope the others might have somehow gotten through?

Oct. 2. After all these dry days of heat and thirst, it has now turned cold and rainy. I long for my woolen shawl left back at the Colorado. Liefy has a bad cough, and Orrin is doing very poorly.

The children leaned together in the wagon, trying to find warmth in the few quilts they had. Mama swaddled Orrin in a blanket like an infant and held him on her lap. The rain soon stopped, and the animals struggled through the mud until they reached La Roux Springs.

"La Roux Springs!" Sallie whispered mournfully. "Remember our last visit here?"

A RAY OF HOPE

Francie nodded sadly and squeezed Sallie's hand. It was here they had lolled together in the meadow, and played in the snow. Oh, to be back in that wonderful time, with Father at their side and their hearts full of hope!

The beautiful green lushness had left La Roux Springs. Now all was brown and desolate. The grass, once long and flowing, crackled beneath their feet like dry, matted straw. The leaves had fallen from the trees, and a sharp wind whistled through the bare branches. That night the children slept curled together in the wagon, their thin quilts scant protection from the frigid air.

The next morning, the eighteen men that everyone had assumed were dead, stumbled into camp, pale and emaciated. Though people rejoiced to know they had not died, once again, this meant no help had been reached. Time was running out.

Now one of Mr. Smith's men that Sallie knew only as "Jake" proposed leading another group out. "It's cool enough to travel both day and night now," he said. "And the recent rain has filled the water holes. We'll press right on through to Albuquerque. We can do it."

Mr. Smith butchered one of his few remaining cows for jerky, and the next day, thirty men set out on horses and mules. With trepidation, Sallie watched them go. Jake, Will Harper, Ed Akey, even Lee Griffin, who now refused to be left behind, all disappeared over the horizon. Would they make it through? If they did, could they reach help in time to save the rest of them?

As Sallie stood watching forlornly, she felt someone touch her shoulder. It was Mr. Udell, with a Bible in his hand. *"Yea, though I walk through the valley of the shadow of death, I will fear no evil,"* the old man quoted softly. *"For thou art with me. Thy rod and thy staff they comfort me."* At that, Sallie leaned her head against the old man's arm and sobbed for a long, long time.

Oct.14. I shivered through the night and found frost on the wagon cover this morning. Liefy and Orrin are still quite sick. It's been ten days since the men left. Mr. Smith says if all is well, they may have reached Zuni pueblo by now.

SALLIE FOX

Late one afternoon, Mr. Smith's last cow dropped dead. He salvaged what he could of its remains, and that night, Sallie ate her allotted portion sitting near the campfire. Glancing around in the flickering firelight, she saw Mama holding Orrin, lying semi-conscious in her arms. Liefy sat bundled in a quilt, taking a cup of hot water from Mrs. Hedgpeth. Francie and Julia shared another quilt, and Ellen sat nearby, cradling her baby cousin in her arms for warmth.

Across the fire sat Mr. Smith, looking uncharacteristically gloomy. Sallie watched him sympathetically. Poor Mr. Smith! He had stayed optimistic longer than anyone else. He'd sacrificed his entire herd, had given everything he had to people he didn't even know, and now sat cold and defeated.

Mrs. Hedgpeth interrupted Sallie's sorrowful reverie. "Have a cup of hot water, my dear," she said. "It will help warm up your insides."

Just then, Sallie heard the unmistakable approach of a wagon and team, and moments later, Jake walked up to their campfire. Mr. Smith yelped with joy, grabbing the man in a bear hug. "I never thought I'd see you alive again!"

"Alive and kicking, sir," Jake happily replied, "and I've got something for you!" Jake whispered something to Mr. Smith, who jubilantly told the others, "The United States government has sent every man, woman, and child of us a month's rations!"

Amidst the group's spontaneous cheer, Mr. Smith waved his hand and continued, "The Freemasons of Albuquerque have sent to Mrs. Alpha Brown...." His voice faltered and he broke down weeping. All Sallie heard was loud sobs throughout the camp. The Masons had sent a special contribution of money and clothing for Mama and the children.

Handing Orrin to Mrs. Hedgpeth, Mama enveloped her daughters in her arms. "My beautiful children," she whispered. "Everyday, I have prayed only that you five children would live. Now it appears my prayer has been answered."

There was happy confusion in camp, as people laughed, cried, and hugged each other. In short order, Jake put a mouthwatering dinner of corn cakes and bacon on the fire. As he cooked, he told them what had happened after the thirty men had set out several weeks before.

"The cool, wet weather made all the difference. We pushed night and day until we reached Zuni pueblo. The Zuni fed and clothed us, and gave us fresh horses. We made it to Albuquerque a week later." Once they'd reached Albuquerque, the military garrison had given them a wagon loaded with supplies, and the Freemasons had added their contribution. Jake and another man had lost no time returning to find the Smith party.

Fortified by an excellent supper and breakfast the next morning, the group set off with renewed vigor. They arrived at Zuni pueblo in two days, and stayed there two more to recover their strength. Ten days later, they reached Albuquerque. But at what should have been their moment of triumph, Sallie's family touched the depths of despair. Orrin died in Mama's arms just as they came in sight of the Rio Grande.

14. THE GILA ROUTE

Sallie stared silently out of the wagon as Mr. Smith drove Mama, the four girls, and the small coffin to a lonesome hillside overlooking the river. They followed another wagon, carrying the Owens family and other Masons Father had met the summer before. When they stopped, Francie helped Sallie climb out of the wagon. Sallie wept as the men lowered the little wooden box into the ground. Mr. Owens recited a prayer, while the men shoveled dirt over the coffin and piled rocks on top of it.

Was Orrin's body really nailed up inside that coffin? Such a small box could never contain her wriggling, spirited brother! Thoughts screamed inside Sallie's head. *It isn't fair. The hard part is over. We're back now, safe from hunger, and cold, and Indians. Why did Orrin die now? It isn't fair.*

Soon, it was time to go. With brimming eyes, Francie helped Sallie climb into the wagon. Julia and Liefy came next, with tear-stained faces. Sallie watched Mama, as Mr. Smith helped her into the wagon. Surprisingly, Mama's eyes were dry and her lips formed the same line of stern determination Sallie had seen every day since August. *Can she still have patience and perseverance in the midst of this?*

Mr. Smith took the reins and turned the wagon around. Suddenly, Mama crumpled in agony. "*My boy, my boy!*" she shrieked in anguish. "How can I leave him back there without me? How can I leave my boy?"

Despite the pain in her side, Sallie flung herself over to Mama, and wrapped her arms around her. Liefy, Francie, and Julia did the same, and the five of them leaned against each other, sobbing. Mr. Smith wiped his own eyes as he drove the wagon back to town.

Nov. 16. We are staying with the Owens family, while Mama decides what to do next. Mrs. Owens gave Liefy special medicine for her cough. I cry for Orrin every day.

Sallie, Julia, and Liefy lay in bed talking, when Mama and Francie came into the room. "We have matters to discuss," Mama said. "Francie and I have just come from Mr. Smith's camp. As you know, he had offered to buy us passage on a wagon train back to Iowa. I have decided not to accept that kind offer. I don't want to go back to Iowa."

"May we stay in Albuquerque?" Sallie asked eagerly. "It's not such a bad place, and the Owens family is so nice." She didn't want to get back into a wagon going anywhere!

"We will stay here a while, Sarah, for you and Relief to recuperate," Mama replied. "But almost all my family is in California, and it's where Father and I had decided to live. *He died trying to get us there.* It's where we belong."

Sallie burst into tears. "But that means crossing the desert again, Mama. And the desert means Indians. Don't make me do it, Mama, I don't want to do it!"

Mama placed her hand on top of Sallie's. "I spoke with Mr. Smith. He has purchased a herd, which he will drive to California this spring. He and his men will not take the Beale Road this time. They will follow the Gila route, which he has traveled before. He will take us with him to Los Angeles, and I'll ask my brother George to meet us there."

"But you said we've imposed too much on Mr. Smith already," Sallie protested. "He sacrificed his cattle for us, and we have no way to pay him back!"

"I *don't* want to impose on Mr. Smith," Mama said. "He has agreed to accept two hundred dollars as payment, which George will give him when we reach Los Angeles." Mama touched Sallie's hair softly. "Don't fret, Sarah. Right now, I just want you to get well."

Dec. 2. Ellen and her mother visited today. It was so good to see them, and to hear news of the others. Most of the men and older boys have found work with the military—either helping build roads or driving supply wagons. Mr. Rose works at a restaurant. Mr. Udell tends cows. Mrs. Udell is quite ill. Ellen herself looks much healthier than the last time I saw her. She says the same of me, though this cold wet weather makes my back ache.

It was chilly and dark when Sallie opened her eyes Christmas morning. She snuggled closer to Mama's sleeping body, for warmth. Suddenly, memories of the previous Christmas in Keosauqua flooded her mind. Sallie could hear Father's jubilant voice saying, "Next year at this time, we'll be in California!" The girls had decorated the house so nicely for the holidays, and Uncle Charles' family had come for dinner. Orrin had ridden around on Father's shoulders, clapping with glee.

Father. Orrin. She missed them so! Gentle tears soon gave way to loud sobs, waking Mama and the others. They all held each other and cried. After a while, Mama dried her eyes. "We have much to be thankful for on this Christmas Day, my dear girls," she reminded them. "We are here, we are alive, Sallie and Liefy are recovering, and Mr. Smith will take us on to California. We must thank God for these blessings, especially today, on His Son's birthday."

Jan. 8, 1859. Mr. Smith now says he doesn't want to wait until spring. We leave tomorrow for Los Angeles. My back still hurts, but I can walk without help now. Ellen and her mother came once more to say good-bye. They hope to continue on to California themselves in a few months.

THE GILA ROUTE

Wearing new dresses Mrs. Owens had sewn for them, and boots and hats from Mr. Owens' store, Sallie and her family waited patiently for Mr. Smith's wagon to come to a full stop. The Owens family stood with them, saying good-bye and promising to look after Orrin's grave. Sallie thought Mama's eyes misted a bit at the mention of his name, but there were no tears. Instead, as they climbed into the wagon, Mama forcefully exclaimed, "Time to go. We're off to California!"

This was a smaller wagon than the one they'd had before, pulled by mules. Jake sat at the reins, while Mr. Smith and the other men herded the cattle on horseback. While they didn't have the protection of a large group, they moved much more quickly than a big wagon train. No more long waits to hitch and unhitch dozens of oxen! They traveled south along the Rio Grande, until they met up with the route followed by the Butterfield Overland Mail, which took them west.

"A Butterfield stagecoach can take a letter from St. Louis, Missouri, to San Francisco in twenty-four days," Mr. Smith told them.

Sallie's jaw dropped. "Twenty-four days!"

"The first Butterfield stage came through here a few months ago, about the time we made it back to Albuquerque. Now, stages come through weekly. We'll probably meet some coming from San Francisco."

Twenty-four days! Sallie could hardly comprehend it. Her family had left Keosauqua eight months ago, and were still far from San Francisco. How could anyone travel that distance in less than a month? Before long, she saw the answer to her question. There were stations set up along the route, often just tents, with several men tending spare horses and preparing food. When a stage pulled into the station, the driver and passengers ate a hasty meal and stretched their legs while the stationmaster hitched up fresh horses. Then it was back on the road, galloping on to the next station, which the stage would reach in hours. Sallie's wagon might cover the same distance in a full day!

Jan. 20. Passing the mail stations helps me feel safer. The stationmasters tell us about the road ahead, and can sell us food if we run out. We don't feel so all alone.

One day, they stopped at the station called Soldier's Farewell Springs. Sallie's legs felt cramped, so Francie helped her walk around a bit to loosen them up. While the mules drank from a trough, Jake filled their water barrel and the girls dipped tin cups in the spring.

"Drink hearty," said the stationmaster, standing nearby. "It's forty-two miles to the next station, with no water along the way. Right in the heart of Apache country, too!"

Sallie dropped her cup in fright at the mention of Apaches.

"Yup," said the stationmaster. "The next station is Stein's Peak. Right before you reach Apache Pass."

Mr. Smith overheard the man talking and came over. "Have the stages been having trouble with the Apaches?"

The stationmaster shrugged. "Nope. The Indians don't seem to pay 'em no nevermind."

"I'm told Chief Cochise stays near Apache Pass when he isn't leading raids into Mexico," Mr. Smith said. Sallie pricked up her ears. She had heard fearsome stories about Cochise from the Owens boys in Albuquerque.

"So they say," the stationmaster replied.

"We're headed for the pass ourselves," Mr. Smith said. "I wonder what we'll find there."

Sallie looked at Mr. Smith with disbelief. "No!" she told him stoutly. "You can't take us there. Not through an Apache hideout. There must be another way!"

Mama hurried over to find Sallie visibly shaking. "He's taking us where the Indians are, Mama, just like at the Colorado. This time we'll all be killed!"

Mr. Smith spoke kindly. "Sallie, I've been this route twice, with no problems. They say Cochise won't hurt Americans, if they don't interfere with his forays into Mexico."

"That offers us cold comfort, Mr. Smith," Mama said ruefully. "We heard the Mojaves would not harm us, either."

"I understand your misgivings, Mrs. Brown," Mr. Smith replied. "However, if you want to go to California, you must pass through Apache country."

Jan. 25. The station at Stein's Pass consists of a tent, a corral, and a spring. No sign of Indians. Tomorrow we enter Apache Pass, a narrow strip through the Dragoon Mountains. My heart is filled with dread.

Sallie looked apprehensively at the steep walls looming up on each side of the wagon. Huge rocks seemed suspended in the air, as if ready to fall any minute. Did Indians lurk behind them? Mama knitted furiously, as Jake steered the mules along the narrow path. Afraid to breathe for fear the sound would somehow bring Apaches flying down upon them, Sallie's stomach tightened like a knot.

Mr. Smith and his men kept the cattle herded as close as possible to the wagon. By late afternoon, they had seen no one. Finally, Mr. Smith rode a little way ahead, searching for water and a place to camp. Descending into a canyon, he disappeared from view.

A short time later, the wagon started down the canyon's narrow path. Jake steered the animals around a bend and then stopped. Mama stifled a scream. Sallie sat bolt upright and looked out the front of the wagon. There stood Mr. Smith, surrounded by about two hundred Apache braves.

Mr. Smith hastened over to the wagon. "Mrs. Brown," he said urgently. "Be strong. Show no fear. Our best hope is to act as naturally as possible."

"Whatever must we do?" Mama whispered.

Mr. Smith flashed her a dazzling smile. "Cook the best meal you're capable of, Mrs. Brown! We have company for supper."

Mama's eyes widened. "We don't have enough cook pots for all these people, not to mention food!"

As though he had heard her, the chief gave a signal, and all but the two braves standing next to him vanished. As Mama and Francie hurried to start supper, Mr. Smith rummaged through the wagon for several red flannel shirts. He presented these to the chief, who seemed pleased with the gift.

Sallie stayed in the wagon with Julia and Liefy. After Mama had served supper to the men, she and Francie brought food for the rest of them. "We must all stay right here until they leave," Mama whispered. "Don't do anything to draw attention."

Every once in a while, Francie peeked through a slit and reported what was going on. "They seem to like Mr. Smith," she said. "They're smoking a peace pipe." Eventually, the Indians left camp, and Sallie and her family tried to sleep. However, being this close to so many Indians made them anxious. The others managed to doze some, but Sallie lay tense and frightened, trying not to relive the horror at the Colorado River in her mind.

The next morning, the same chief and two braves returned, and Mr. Smith offered them breakfast. After they'd eaten, Sallie watched timidly from the wagon, as Mama cleaned up with shaking hands. Would the Indians let them leave? When all was packed to go, the chief stepped forward, and handed Mr. Smith a quiver of arrows and a highly ornamented bow. Using a combination of sign language and bits of Spanish, the chief said if he was ever approached by Apaches, he should show them the quiver, which was marked by the sign of Cochise.

Cochise! Their dinner guest had been that famous chief! Mr. Smith solemnly accepted these gifts, and to everyone's relief, the Indians disappeared into the canyon. After they'd left, Mr. Smith turned to the others with a nervous laugh. "I think Cochise was impressed by my bald head. He seemed to think I had survived a scalping!" Jake hitched up the mules, and they left Apache Pass as quickly as possible.

Slowly they plodded onward. Sometimes the desolate landscape gave way to coarse salt grass or cactus plants towering twelve feet in the air. They passed through the small village of Tucson, and several days later, reached the Gila River. Sallie saw clusters of mud huts surrounded by acres of well-cultivated farmland.

"It's called the Pima Villages," said Mr. Smith. "It's similar to Zuni Pueblo. This will be a good place to stay for a few days."

Feb. 5. The Pima houses look like mud beehives. The people raise wheat, corn, and melons. The women wear a kind of cloth skirt, but above the waist, they wear beads around their neck and nothing else.

Despite her pain, Sallie found herself able to walk longer distances without help. During their stay at the Pima Villages, she and Francie enjoyed strolling along the banks of the Gila River. Though still full of sorrow about the events of the previous year, the girls felt hopeful about the future.

"When we get to Aunt Julia's, I don't want to go anywhere else again," Sallie said emphatically. "I will settle in one spot and grow roots, just like a big old tree!" Just then, she looked down at her feet and noticed some strange looking rocks. Picking them up, she realized they weren't rocks at all. "Walnuts!" she exclaimed. "Francie, these look like walnuts!"

Francie studied them closely. "They do look like walnuts! I know the Pima grow lots of things, but I don't see walnut trees anywhere around here."

Later, Sallie showed them to Mr. Smith. "They're walnuts all right, but how did they get on the banks of the Gila?" he said, scratching his bald head. "Maybe someone brought them from back east, and they somehow fell out of a wagon."

"I think they are good luck charms," Sallie said triumphantly. "I'm going to keep them in my pocket, and plant them at Uncle Si's ranch in California. Maybe I'll get my tree after all!"

15. CALIFORNIA

Two weeks past the Pima Villages, they reached the spot where the Gila River joined up with the Colorado. Tears stung Sallie's eyes, as she remembered the last time she had looked at the waters of this river. That had been two hundred miles upstream, when they had buried Father in it. The family stared at the river for several silent moments, until Francie pointed to its far bank, saying, "There's California. Again."

Feb. 19. Yuma Crossing. Tomorrow we shall pass over this last barrier by ferry, leaving New Mexico Territory for good. I shall not miss it! How I wish Father could step triumphantly into California with us.

When Sallie heard people calling the ferryman "Don Diego," she assumed he was Mexican. To her surprise, "Don Diego" was a tall, blond, and blue-eyed American, whose actual name was Jaeger, which the locals found hard to pronounce.

"Are you the little girl who was shot with an arrow?" Don Diego asked her when they finally met. When she nodded, he stuck out a heavily scarred arm. "I took two arrows here and another two right here." He pointed to a similar scar across the back of his neck. "Healed completely. I'm in perfect health right now." Sallie inspected the scars carefully, wondering if her own would look like that some day.

"Up until nine years ago, there was no easy way to cross the Colorado right here," Mr. Jaeger explained. "I changed that." He'd left Philadelphia in 1848, he told her, sailing round the Horn to San Francisco. Then, he became a cook on one of the first steamer boats to run the Colorado River, reaching this spot in July, 1850. "That's when some Quechan Indians ambushed me, giving me these scars. But it didn't stop me from starting my own ferry service, store, and now, a Butterfield stage station. And don't you let your misfortunes stop you from accomplishing everything you want to do, either!"

The Smith party didn't dally in the town Mr. Jaeger called Arizona City. Mama mailed Uncle George another letter, saying they hoped to reach Los Angeles in mid-March. "The Butterfield stage should get this letter to him in plenty of time for him to meet us there," Mama said.

Then Mr. Jaeger carried their wagon and team across the Colorado on a flatboat, and made several more trips for the cattle. Once on the other side, Francie pointed back across the river, saying, "I don't want to see that place again as long as I live!" Sallie agreed wholeheartedly.

But, although they had finally reached California, they still faced weeks of travel. How Sallie wished she could move as fast as the letter to Uncle George! Heavy sand made the first sixty miles beyond the Colorado River difficult. Everyone except Sallie walked beside the wagon, to lighten the load. Some of the sand drifts were so high, they entirely covered the road. "Sand can be worse to get through than snow," a stationmaster told them. "During one sandstorm last year, a rancher lost three thousand head of sheep in six hours."

No sandstorms beset them, however, and in a few days they found themselves at the edge of a saltwater lake. Walking along the shoreline with her sisters, Sallie found some ancient seashells. She placed them in her pocket with the nuts she'd found on the banks of the Gila.

Finally, they left the desert behind them. The road became a happy blur of beautiful weather and stunning scenery. They stopped for water at Warner's Ranch, on the eastern edge of San Diego County. Turning north, they passed through a corner of San Bernardino County, with the towering San Bernardino Mountains to one side, and the coastal range to the other. Nearing Los Angeles, they stopped to visit San Gabriel Mission, its lush gardens and vineyards surrounded by fruit-laden orange trees.

Before long, Sallie stood on a hilltop overlooking Los Angeles, a picturesque little town with flat-roofed adobe houses. Beyond it stretched a green, level plain, and far beyond that, the gleaming Pacific Ocean. Sallie drank in the magnificent sight, and then turned to Liefy. "*Father would have loved this!*"

Squeezing her hand, Liefy replied, "I'm sure he's in heaven, and I'm sure he knows we are here now. How happy that must make him!"

They pulled into Los Angeles, and Mr. Smith rented them a room for the night near the town plaza. Suddenly, as if by magic, Uncle George Baldwin was there with them. He wept with joy to see his sister again, and scooped the girls into his loving arms. He also brought happy news: Aunt Livinia had married last year and was now with child!

"Vini, married!" Mama exclaimed. "When? To whom?"

"To a blacksmith in Placerville," George laughed. "See how much can happen when you are out of touch for a whole year?"

March 15. Uncle George is every bit as much fun as I remembered. We shall leave tomorrow for Uncle Si's. Mr. Smith will stay here to sell his cattle. I shall miss this dear man almost as much as I do Father.

Sallie overheard Uncle George speaking to Mr. Smith, as the family prepared to say their good-byes. "There's no way I can adequately thank you for bringing my sister and nieces safely here," he said. "The news of their ordeal rent our hearts! Thank you, kind sir, for the protection and service you gave them."

"They've come to be as dear to my heart as my own family back home, Mr. Baldwin. I was glad to help."

Uncle George took out a small packet from a leather case. "Here's two hundred dollars my sister asked me to bring you."

Mr. Smith shook his head. "I never intended to take any money from you, Mr. Baldwin. I mentioned that sum to Mrs. Brown only to ease her concern. She worried so much about being a burden."

"I would gladly pay many times that amount!"

"Please, Mr. Baldwin. Your sister must start a new life for herself and her children. Use the money to help them get settled in a new home."

Soon, Uncle George's wagon was ready to go. Mama shook Mr. Smith's hand warmly, thanking him over and over for all he had done for them. Francie, Julia, and Liefy hugged and thanked him, promising to write.

Sallie hung back, too overcome with emotion to speak. Finally, tears streaming down her face, she threw her arms around him and cried, "I shall never forget you, Mr. Smith! I shall always remember those sunbonnets coming over the canyon wall, and the handsome man who saved my life. When I grow up and get married, I shall name my first son after you!"

Mr. Smith looked her in the eye and said solemnly, "Sallie, nothing would honor me more than that. Thank you."

Then he stood on the walkway of the Los Angeles town plaza, waving, as Uncle George urged the mules forward. Sallie sat in the back of the wagon, waving back, until they turned a corner. Sighing aloud, she said, "He is a good man and we are so lucky he found us!"

May 17. The Pacific Ocean sparkles in the distance as I write this. It is the biggest thing I've ever seen! Uncle George says we will walk on the beach near Mission San Buenaventura.

Uncle George stopped the wagon, and Francie, Julia, and Liefy ran out to the edge of the surf. Because Sallie's back was hurting, she lagged behind with Mama. George put one arm around his sister, and another around Sallie, gazing out at the beautiful blue ocean. Mama muttered under her breath, "Finally. There's enough of it."

"What did you say, Mary?"

"*Water*, George, water," Mama replied firmly. "When we were stuck in that infernal desert, I thought I would never see enough water again." She gave her brother a tired smile. "But there it is, enough water."

Beyond San Buenaventura, their path followed the coast, and then swung inland through the state's vast central valley. The days went quickly, with Uncle George repeating family stories and telling them about life in California. As Sallie gazed out at the grasses and wildflowers, as she watched the birds, she remembered those exciting days at the beginning of the Santa Fe Trail. She had wound flower garlands for her hair, dreaming of California! Now, here she was, in the very heart of it.

Sallie looked around the wagon at her family. As much as she missed Father and Orrin, she felt a glow of appreciation for these smiling faces surrounding her. They had been through so much together, and they had survived! She watched Mama joking with Uncle George, happy and relaxed for the first time in months. Francie and Julia looked strong and healthy, and the color had come back to Liefy's cheeks. Sallie put her hand on her own torso. Even the pain in her side had receded during the past few days. Right then, she knew that like Don Diego, she would heal from her wounds. She owed it to Father to live the wonderful life in California he had always envisioned for her!

On April 3, exactly one year after leaving Keosauqua, they reached Uncle Si's ranch in Vacaville. After all the family members had been hugged and kissed, and the events of the previous year had been thoroughly explained, Sallie reached into her pocket to show Uncle Si the mysterious nuts she'd found on the banks of the Gila River. Uncle Si examined them carefully. "They're walnuts, sure enough," he said. "Let's plant them together, Sallie, to commemorate all you've been through to get here." Then, with Uncle Si leading the way, Sallie limped over to a spot that seemed just perfect for planting a nut tree.

Epilogue: One of the nuts Sallie planted grew to be a big walnut tree, which for many years offered shade to travelers on old Highway 40 in Vacaville. The tree itself is gone now, but a restaurant and shopping complex called The Nut Tree stood on that spot for seventy-five years. It was owned by descendents of Josiah and Julia Allison.

Sallie's mother settled the family in Placerville, and in 1860 married for a third time, having two more children. Relief Brown took ill and died a few years after reaching California. Francie, Julia, and Sallie all grew to adulthood, married, and had children of their own. Sallie, a school teacher in San Francisco, married a man named Oliver Perry Allen. True to her promise, she named her son "E.O." after Mr. Smith. She also had a daughter named Edith, who later wrote down many of the stories her mother told her about this trip.

Mr. Smith returned to Illinois, but eventually brought his family to California, where he became a prominent farmer and statesman in San Jose. When he died in 1892, Sallie gave a eulogy at his memorial service, speaking movingly about the important role he had played in her life.

Mr. Rose's family went to Santa Fe, and eventually to southern California, where he raised oranges, grapes, and racehorses, and became a member of the California State Legislature. A son born after he reached California wrote a book about his father's life.

A few months after Sallie's family left Albuquerque, the Hedgpeths and the Udells embarked once more upon the Beale Wagon Road. This time, Lieutenant Beale himself escorted them, accompanied by fifty men hired by the government to improve road conditions along that route. John Udell reached California in June, 1859. Several months later, he published a journal that remains the most complete chronicle of these events available.

SALLIE FOX

The Baleys went to California the following year, probably also by the Beale Wagon Road, which by that time had become a major westward route for travelers.

The various cattle hands apparently lost their taste for California, and turned their sights back home. They earned money for the return trip by working for the U.S. government in New Mexico, hauling supplies to military posts. Most arrived back in the states shortly before the outbreak of the Civil War. After working as a schoolteacher, Will Harper joined the Union forces, and was killed in battle. Lee Griffin fought for the Confederacy, and was also killed. Ed Akey survived the war, and lived to be an old man. In 1915, at the age of 83, Akey told his version of the Mojave attack and the desert ordeal to a newspaper man from the Keosauqua Reporter.

No one knows for sure why the Mojaves attacked the group at the river. However, the Indians had ample reason to feel encroached upon by white settlers. Several government expeditions, including Lieutenant Beale's, had passed through during the previous year. It must have seemed very threatening when the Rose train arrived with its vast herd and started cutting down trees. But while the Mojaves succeeded in driving this group away, their victory was short-lived. The Beale Road became a major thoroughfare, and the U.S. government built Fort Mojave nearby to protect it. The government also eventually established the Mojave Indian reservation, and forced the tribe to live there.

Although Cochise had a reputation as one of the most brutal and feared Apaches, at the time the Smith party met him, he was trying to get along with the Americans. That would change later, when for ten years he waged war against the U.S. military. Eventually defeated, he spent his last days on a reservation.

Lieutenant Edward Beale was appointed Surveyor General of California by President Abraham Lincoln. Beale built himself an immense ranch near Fort Tejon, providing a haven for many of the camels that had crossed the country during his grand experiment.

The walnut Sallie planted grew to be a huge tree. In 1921, Josiah Allison's grandchildren opened a fruit stand in the shade of its immense branches. That small shack grew into a large complex that included a restaurant, stores, and a private airport. The original tree no longer exists, but there are others on the property that grew from its walnuts. Photo courtesy The Nut Tree.

Sallie's name on the rock at El Morro National Monument, New Mexico. Photo by Reggie Wallace.

Mr. and Mrs. John Udell. It's unknown whether this is his first wife, Emily, who died sometime after reaching California, or Mrs. Clarinder Anderson, the woman he married after Emily's death.

John Udell's journal remains the most complete record of Sallie's journey in existence. (Photo courtesy C. Melvin Bliven.)

The dress Sallie was wearing during the Mojave attack still bears an arrow hole in the torso area. Its skirt is short —Mama cut part of it off to make Sallie a sunbonnet. Photo by Teresa Willis.

ACKNOWLEDGEMENTS AND SOURCES

I first learned about Sallie Fox from a menu note at the Nut Tree restaurant in Vacaville, California. Intrigued, I sought out Shawn Lum, of the Nut Tree staff, who told me more of Sallie's story. She gave me various materials, and put me in touch with Mrs. Leona Crownover, Sallie's great-great-granddaughter. Mrs. Crownover generously provided copies of family records and documents, along with the photo of Sallie included here.

Library research turned up a published volume of a journal kept by John Udell, which formed the basis for this book. However, using literary license, I made the words Sallie's instead.

L.J. Rose of Sunny Slope, a history of the Rose family, provided much useful background. Memoirs by Joel Hedgpeth, Jr., and Sallie's sister Julia (under the pen name of Kate Heath) added extra details. I also consulted many books about the Santa Fe Trail and the history of the American southwest. *Land of Enchantment: Memoirs of Marion Russell along the Santa Fe Trail*, chronicles the experiences of a young girl who traveled the trail about the time Sallie did. I drew heavily on it for a child's perspective of life on a wagon train.

I am indebted to Jack Beale Smith, for the information in his various books about the Beale Wagon Road; to Charles Baley, who gave valuable information and telephone support; to C. Melvin Bliven, for the photo of his great-great-grandfather, John Udell; to Reggie Wallace, formerly a ranger at El Morro National Monument, who photographed Sallie's signature on the rock. Thanks are also due to Alan Hitz, archivist at the Santa Fe Trail Center in Larned, Kansas, and the research staffs of the Arizona Historical Society and the San Jose Historical Society. Much gratitude goes to Judith Ross Enderle and Stephanie Gordon Tessler, of Writers Ink; to Diane Wilde, of Wolfe Design Group; to Teresa Willis; to Leslie Batson; to Mary Bourguignon, for incalculable assistance; to my mother, Dorothy Mary Kupcha, for eagle-eyed copy editing; to my children, Jeremy and Rachel, who light up my life; and most of all, to my wonderful husband, Bob, for love, support, inspiration, and editorial help.

Dorothy Kupcha Leland

Also from Tomato Enterprises:

Read about the adventure of another pioneer girl!

Patty Reed's Doll
The Story of the Donner Party

By Rachel K. Laurgaard

In the winter of 1846, a group of pioneers known as the Donner Party was stranded by heavy snows in the Sierra Nevada Mountains. They endured bitter hardships while

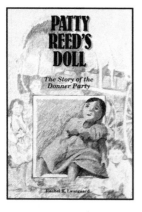

trapped for months without food, unable to continue their westward journey to California. Many of them died in the struggle. But certain ones survived, including eight-year-old Patty Reed, a little girl filled with dignity and determination in the face of mortal danger.

This book is Patty's story, as told by Dolly, the tiny wooden doll she kept hidden in her dress. Dolly vividly remembers days on the prairies and nights around the campfire. She recalls Indian tribes they encountered, and the dusty, tiresome trek through the desert. During the bleak snowbound months, Dolly was Patty's only comfort. Pieced together from letters, journals and memoirs of Donner Party survivors, *Patty Reed's Doll* is the heartwarming tale of how a little girl's love for her doll can transcend all danger.

ISBN 0-9617357-2-4 $7.95